"When you get married to the prince, can we be in your wedding?"

Lily held the picture book *Snow White* in one hand, her other hand clutching Sabrina's arm.

The other children nodded vigorously.

"Please," they said.

"Can we?"

"We'll be good."

"Say yes!"

Sabrina couldn't say no. So she said yes. She didn't want to explain that the chances of her getting married, let alone to a prince, were almost zero.

When she walked into the living room, she saw that Zach had made a fire in the hearth.

The scene was too perfect. Kids all tucked into their beds and a man waiting in front of a blazing fire. Yesterday she was a runaway bride. Today she'd fallen into a fairy-tale scenario. One that she'd only dreamed about. And even though she knew it wasn't real, she wished this fantasy would never end.

Dear Reader,

Icy winds and fierce snowstorms have nothing on this month's heroines who all seem to have a score to settle. And you know the old line about hell having no fury like a woman scorned—well, grab a hot drink and a comfortable chair and watch what happens when these women dole out their best shots!

Alice Sharpe leads off the month with the final installment in the PERPETUALLY YOURS trilogy. In *A Tail of Love* (#1806), it takes one determined wire fox terrier to convince his stubborn mistress to *stay* with the man she left two years ago. Ever since the big man on campus jilted her in high school, a former plain Jane has wanted revenge…and now his return, her transformation and a bachelor auction provide the perfect opportunity in Teresa Southwick's *In Good Company* (#1807)—the second book in her BUY-A-GUY miniseries. Realizing her groom will always put his work first, a runaway bride heads for the mountains and lands on the doorstep of a man who could give her the storybook ending she craves, in Carol Grace's *Snow White Bride* (#1808), part of her charming FAIRY-TALE BRIDES series. Finally, a computer programmer devises the perfect matchmaking program to exact revenge on her new boss, but she quickly finds that even the best-laid computer program can't account for human attraction, in Judith McWilliams's scintillating romance, *The Matchmaking Machine* (#1809).

Happy reading.

Ann Leslie Tuttle
Associate Senior Editor

Please address questions and book requests to:
Silhouette Reader Service
U.S.: 3010 Walden Ave., P.O. Box 1325, Buffalo, NY 14269
Canadian: P.O. Box 609, Fort Erie, Ont. L2A 5X3

Snow White Bride

CAROL GRACE

Fairy Tale Brides

SILHOUETTE *Romance*®

Published by Silhouette Books

America's Publisher of Contemporary Romance

SILHOUETTE BOOKS

ISBN 0-373-19808-6

SNOW WHITE BRIDE

Visit Silhouette Books at www.eHarlequin.com

Printed in U.S.A.

Books by Carol Grace

Silhouette Romance

*Miramar Inn
†Best-Kept Wishes
**Fairy-Tale Brides

CAROL GRACE

has always been interested in travel and living abroad. She spent her junior year of college in France and toured the world working on the hospital ship *HOPE*. She and her husband spent the first year and a half of their marriage in Iran, where they both taught English. She has studied Arabic and Persian languages. Then, with their toddler daughter, they lived in Algeria for two years.

Carol says that writing is another way of making her life exciting. Her office is her mountaintop home, which overlooks the Pacific Ocean and which she shares with her inventor husband, their daughter, who just graduated college, and their teenage son.

For Judy Sullivan who reads all my
books and catches all the mistakes, and
Susan Sandler, for all the laughs dating back to college
days. Good friends like you are hard to find!
Thanks for the good times.
Here's to many more.

Chapter One

It was Sabrina White's wedding day.

And the groom was a no-show.

The church was full of friends and relatives who must be getting impatient by now. But not as impatient as Sabrina, who paced back and forth in the church vestibule while her bridesmaids chattered nervously and her stepmother looked out the window. The scent of the stephanotis in her bouquet was suddenly cloying. The white silk dress that had fit perfectly an hour ago was now too tight, too long and cut too low. She tugged at the neckline and checked her diamond-encrusted watch for the umpteenth time. Adam was impossibly, inexcusably late. Again.

Last night, he'd arrived at the rehearsal dinner an hour and a half late. He'd had an excuse prepared. He always did.

"Couldn't help it, babe," he'd said, kissing her on the cheek. "I'm in the middle of something big. Really important."

She didn't doubt it. He was always in the middle of something bigger and more important than her. A business deal. He'd missed her birthday and skipped Christmas due to business. He even answered cell phone calls in the middle of a kiss. But when he looked deep into her eyes and swore he'd change, she wanted to believe him. He'd said things would be different once they were married. Once he got this deal sewn up. If only she'd hang on until he made partner. Kids? Sure, after they were financially secure. Time alone together? Once they left for their honeymoon.

If they left for their honeymoon. *If* he made it to the wedding. *If* she forgave him one more time. She sighed and glanced at her watch again. It was two-thirty. The ceremony was supposed to have started at two. The organist had played her entire repertoire at least three times.

There was another wedding scheduled at four at the popular church atop San Francisco's Nob Hill. Sabrina could just imagine the next bride arriving as they were leaving, rice thrown at her by mistake, their guests mingling. She tried to stay calm, but the scene she conjured in her mind caused an hysterical giggle to bubble up and escape her lips.

Her stepmother gave her a startled look and adjusted her veil. "Don't worry. He's on his way," Genevieve said calmly.

Sabrina pressed her lips together to keep from blurting something she'd regret. Something like, "How do you know?" Or, "He's always on his way." Or, "I can't take it anymore. I'll give him ten more minutes and then…" And then what? Then she'd walk out? And go where? And do what? She couldn't do that. What would people say?

"Your father's the same way," Genevieve said. "Always late. You don't know what they go through, the pressures, the high stakes, the money involved. You have to understand that's what it takes to succeed in this world—dedication, long hours, hard work and an occasional missed appointment."

She would hardly equate her wedding to an appointment! But Genevieve was wrong. Sabrina understood why her father had never been around when she was growing up. Never home for dinner, gone early in the morning. Golfing with clients on the weekends. Even when he had been home, he was on the phone for hours. It was dedication, all right. Dedication to the firm and not to his family. Sabrina still believed her mother's frail health wasn't helped any by her father's lifestyle. When she'd died when Sabrina was twelve, her father re-married within the year.

Sabrina scanned her stepmother's perfect features, made more perfect by recent Botox in-jections. They had a cordial relationship. Gene-vieve had never tried to be a mother to Sabrina, thinking of herself as more of a big sister. A slightly bossy big sister, in Sabrina's opinion.

Of course, Genevieve didn't mind her father's schedule. She expected it. She expected the money and the social status. She expected a McMansion and an expensive car or two and a vacation house at Lake Tahoe. She'd traded companionship for security. What else had she traded? Sabrina met Genevieve's serene gaze and realized she'd never know.

If Sabrina married Adam, she could expect the same. She'd be secure. She wouldn't have to worry about money. But Adam's behavior wouldn't end at their honeymoon. Or with his closing this deal or being made partner. Because she knew in her heart he wouldn't change. Was that the kind of life she wanted?

Was Adam the kind of husband she wanted?

Suddenly her life stretched ahead of her like a long, empty highway and she felt a chill permeate her body. She knew the answers to her questions. She knew what she had to do. It was now or never.

A calm born of desperation overtook her. She said to her stepmother, "I'm going to the bathroom." She was going farther than the bathroom. She had no idea where, but somewhere far away from this farce of a wedding.

In the hall, she bumped into her best friend and maid of honor in her pale pink dress and matching shoes.

"Meg," she said, "I have to leave. Can you help me?"

"Leave? You can't leave now." Meg put her hands on Sabrina's shoulders. "You're getting married in—" she glanced at her watch and frowned "—soon."

"No, I'm not. I can't marry Adam. Not today, not ever. Can I borrow your car?"

"Of course, but where are you going?"

"I don't know. Somewhere far away."

Meg raised her eyebrows. "Are you sure you want to do this?"

Sabrina took a deep breath. "I'm sure."

"But how will you—explain it to the guests, to Adam?"

"I don't know how." Sabrina shivered. Her mouth was dry, her knees were weak. She'd never been so scared in her life, or so sure of anything. "But I'll think of something. Maybe the truth."

"I know you're upset, but—"

"I'm more than upset. If I don't leave now, I'll regret it for the rest of my life."

Meg's eyes widened. Then she pressed her car keys into Sabrina's hand.

Sabrina felt her eyes fill with grateful tears. "You're the best friend anyone could have. I owe you for this. I'll make it up to you somehow. Remember that. Anything you want. Anything at all."

"Don't worry about it. Just call and let me know you're okay."

Sabrina nodded. All she had to do was walk

down the hall and out the side door into the parking lot, get into Meg's black BMW and go.

Go where?

It didn't matter.

Would her family worry? Of course, but they'd understand. They had to. She just needed some time to figure things out. One thing she knew, she was not going to marry anyone until she found a man who put home and family before a fancy house or an expensive sports car. Someone who wanted lots of kids and was willing to help bring them up. Did such a man exist? If he didn't, she'd spend the rest of her life taking care of other people's kids in the classroom.

It was almost too easy, she thought as she got into the car and pulled out into the street. No one saw her. The parking lot was full of cars, but no people. All the guests were inside and seated. And the groom? He was on his way. And she was on *her* way. Wouldn't it be funny if they passed each other on the street going in opposite directions and didn't realize it?

She gripped the steering wheel tightly, watching the traffic, but she didn't see Adam's midnight blue Porsche. She heaved a sigh of relief. If she ran into him, he might try to change her mind. Try to sweet-talk her into going through with it, though she knew deep down she shouldn't and wouldn't.

Adam wouldn't believe she was walking out on him. He expected her to be waiting for him, no matter the time. He'd never understand her running out of patience. But she'd warned him. She'd told him how she felt about his being late or not showing up for things that were important to her. Apparently it had never sunk in how much it bothered her.

She headed instinctively for the Golden Gate Bridge and then drove northeast toward the Sierra Nevadas, where she'd spent winter holidays as a child and summers at camp learning to kayak and make beaded lanyards. Those were the days, simpler times when mistakes didn't have such dire consequences.

She just needed a few days to herself, in a place where she'd once been happy. She thought of the clear, crisp mountain air, the sound of the wind in the trees, the stars at night so close you could almost touch them.

Her idea was to stop at a lodge high in the mountains. She'd check in under an assumed name, in case her father or stepmother or Adam came looking for her.

They'd try to persuade her to come back and face the music—"The Wedding March," to be exact. They'd tell her she'd embarrassed herself—and them—in front of everyone they knew, which was no doubt true. They'd tell her she had wedding jitters, nothing more, and that everyone had them. That she'd get over it. But she wouldn't. She'd done the right thing. She felt it in her bones. She'd done it a little late, yes, but better late than never.

Three hours later, as she wound her way up a narrow mountain road, the sun was setting, the temperature was dropping and snow was lightly falling. Outside, it was picture-postcard pretty November day. But inside the car in her wedding dress, Sabrina was cold, even with the heater turned up full force. She could hardly wait to get out of this dress and into a warm sweater and stretch pants that she would purchase at a ski shop and sip a hot spiced cider in front of a blazing fire. Okay, maybe she did appreciate some of the comforts money could buy.

But where was this charming lodge she'd imagined? She was too tired to go much farther. She'd have to settle for an ordinary motel for the night.

As she made a sharp U-turn to return to the small town of Piney Ridge, the car's front wheel landed in a ditch on the side of the road. She pressed her foot against the accelerator. The engine roared, but the wheels only spun in place.

Damn, damn, damn. Well, she'd really done it now. She was free. She'd escaped. But she was stranded on a deserted road, dressed for a wedding instead of the weather. And no one knew where she was.

Okay, no need for panic. She'd walk back to the house she'd passed and ask to use the phone. Then she'd call a taxi, have the car towed and find herself a place to stay.

That settled, she unbuckled her seat belt and slid up the seat to open the car door.

The snow was falling faster and heavier as she trudged down the road in her white dress and *peau de soie* wedding shoes. The house was farther than she thought. She was numb from the cold, her teeth chattered, and the flakes stung her skin, but she kept going. She had no choice. She had not made the most important decision of her life only to be found frozen in the snow weeks later.

It seemed like hours before she reached the house, light blazing from every window, in a thicket of pine trees at the end of a long driveway. Her feet raw, her dress soaked, she flung herself at the front door and rapped on it with frozen fingers. "Please, somebody, answer the door. Let me in." Her voice cracked.

When the door finally opened, Sabrina opened her mouth to speak, but no words came out. Her lips were numb. Her vision was blurred. She must have been delirious, because she thought she saw seven children and a tall, handsome man standing behind them. A house full of kids with a man who stayed home to take care of them? She'd succumbed to the elements. She'd died and gone to heaven. She took a step forward and then fell in a heap onto the floor.

The last thing she remembered was hearing piping little voices.

"She came!"

"I told you she would."

"It's really her. It's Snow White!"

Chapter Two

For one crazy minute, Zach thought the kids might be right. She looked like Snow White, with her dark hair, pale skin and perfect features—not to mention the white dress. At least like the illustration in the book they begged him to read every night since his brother left him with this madhouse three days ago.

Whoever she was, wherever she came from, she needed help. He scooped the woman up off the floor, yelled at the kids to close the door, find a blanket, get a hot water bottle, look for warm clothes, bring towels. Excited by the arrival of

"Snow White," for once they didn't question his orders.

They scattered in different directions, leaving him alone holding the woman in his arms, her head on his shoulder, her wet clothes plastered to her body. He felt an unaccustomed surge of protectiveness. He was used to women who were completely self-sufficient, not one who fainted and certainly not one who appeared at a stranger's door in a low-cut white dress that was hardly appropriate garb for early winter in the Sierras.

Gently, he set her on the couch and reached for the cell phone in his pocket. His brother had entered the pediatrician's number in it before he left. Surely any doctor could tell him what to do for the woman.

In a few minutes, he was connected to the nurse.

"You say she was outside but not dressed for the weather?" the nurse asked.

"All she's wearing is a white dress. A wet white dress."

"Probably hypothermia. Have her take off those wet clothes. Right away."

"Uh…there's a problem. She fainted."

"Could be from the shock of her body's temperature change. Get that dress off of her."

"But I don't even know her—"

"Now!"

"Okay, okay. Hold on. Don't go away."

Zach set the phone down and began fumbling with a score of tiny buttons from the dress's neckline to the waist. He was breathing hard when he saw her creamy breasts were revealed, only half concealed by a white lace demibra. When he pulled the dress over her head and tossed it on a chair, he saw she was wearing a matching bikini. He knew expensive underwear when he saw it. He knew sexy underwear, too, and this was definitely sexy and expensive. Where had she been going in this underwear and white wedding dress? The answer was obvious. To a wedding. *Her* wedding.

He wrenched her wet shoes off, tossed them across the floor and grabbed a hand-knit afghan throw to wrap her in.

He picked up the phone again. "Okay, I've got the dress off and she's covered up. What else should I do if she's got hypothermia?"

"What we look for is the 'umbles," the nurse explained. "Stumbles, mumbles, fumbles and grumbles. Does she exhibit any of those symptoms?"

"All she's done so far is pass out."

"What about her skin, is it cold and pale?"

"That's right, cold and pale—like porcelain."

"Another thing. Listen to her breathe. A very slow rate is not a good sign. Why don't you check out her breathing, take her temperature and call me back. If it's under 96 and she's having trouble breathing, we're in trouble and you should call 911."

Zach's heart lurched. *Trouble. 911.* He hung up, raced to the bathroom and found a thermometer in the medicine chest.

Where were those kids? He wondered as he returned to the unconscious woman. He could hear them yelling at one another, hear their footsteps as they raced up and down the stairs. No doubt they were enjoying the novelty of the situation, which was more than he could say. He'd had enough novelty since he'd arrived here only a few days ago to last him for years.

After shaking the thermometer, Zach gently slid it between the woman's lips and under her tongue. Her eyelashes fluttered, but she didn't protest.

Where were those kids? All day they hadn't left him alone for a minute. Now that he needed them, they'd disappeared.

He lowered his head over the woman's face.

Her breathing was slow, but not too slow. It was even and seemed to match his own. Since he was a fit thirty-three-year-old, that had to be a good sign.

"Lily, Mary Ann, Brendan, Michael, Jack, Jenny and Millie," he called. "Where are you? Get in here."

They came running with a blanket, a towel, a glass of water, a box of crackers, the hot water bottle, a large sweater and sweatpants.

"Is she awake?" towheaded Millie asked, hopping from one foot to the other.

"Is she alive?" Mary Ann wanted to know, gnawing on her fingernails, perhaps remembering that a neighbor had died in a gang-related gunfight before she was taken into foster care.

"Of course she's alive," Zach assured them all.

"Is she gonna stay with us?" Jack asked hopefully. He missed Doreen badly and was probably afraid she wasn't coming back. Who could blame the little guy after the series of foster parents before Al and Doreen.

But stay with them? That was all he needed, a strange, mysterious woman who'd appeared out of nowhere staying with them. If the woman would only wake up, she'd most likely be on her way to wherever she was supposed to be going.

"Can she read us a story?" Jenny asked hopefully, waving a slim picture book in her hand. As if they hadn't heard enough stories.

He'd read to them nonstop since he'd arrived, not only about Snow White, but about trucks and trailers and trains and princesses and goblins and witches.

"Can we go out and play in the snow?" Michael, the five year old who was small for his age, was the active one, never holding still, always running, jumping, falling, tumbling. Zach had no idea how his sister-in-law coped with this group. Sure, some went to school. Sure, his brother was home at night after work and on weekends. Still, how did they keep any semblance of order around the house? He sure hadn't been able to.

Instead of trying to answer all their questions— a challenge for any confirmed bachelor thrust into a houseful of active kids and especially for him— Zach told Lily to drape the soft wool blanket she'd brought from her bed across Snow White's feet. Then he lifted Ms. White's head and instructed Jenny to slip the towel she was clutching under their guest's wet hair.

The girls were wide-eyed and quiet as they stared at the sleeping figure. He saw the rapt expressions on the faces of the boys as they, too, gazed at the woman on the couch. It had taken the arrival of a woman out of a fairy tale to finally stun them into complete silence for the first time since he'd arrived.

Zach removed the thermometer from Snow White's mouth and held it up to the light. Ninety-seven. He breathed a sigh of relief.

"Is she sick?" Brendan asked, his little face scrunched in a frown. He'd been sick a lot himself, Zach knew. In and out of hospitals before his brother had taken him in, he was thin but otherwise looked healthy, no doubt due to the good care Al and Doreen lavished on all these kids.

"I think she's just tired," Zach explained.

"And cold," Jenny said, touching Snow White lightly on the arm.

"Don't touch her," Lily warned. As the oldest, she was used to giving orders. Whether anyone followed them was another matter.

"She's cold, all right. But she's warming up now, thanks to you guys," Zach assured them.

They grinned at him. Then Mary Ann and Jenny sat on the carpet while Brendan, Jack and Michael flung themselves down on the floor next to the girls. Lily put one hand on Zach's shoulder and leaned against him. She was eight going on

eighteen, a sweet little kid who took her respon-
sibilities of caring for the little ones seriously.

For three days, there'd been nothing but noise
and chaos from the seven of them. Then this beautiful woman knocks on the door and conks out in
their living room. Just what he needed in the
middle of babysitting and trying to deal with a
crisis at his company one hundred and fifty miles
away.

He'd requested a temporary nanny from a local
agency, but he didn't think they came on foot
wearing three-inch satin heels in the middle of a
snowstorm. So who was she?

With the bribe of some microwave popcorn, he
got the kids to give Snow White her privacy and
closed the door to the living room.

"Okay, kids," he said as he ushered them into
the den, "let's put a video on. What'll it be?" he
asked, pointing to the shelf above the TV. As if he
didn't know.

"*Snow White*. Let's watch *Snow White*," Lily
said, her eyes shining with anticipation.

"I'm hungry," Brendan said. That started an
argument over food versus the video. A wrestling
match broke out between Brendan and Michael
until Zach yanked the boys apart and said they

could watch and eat at the same time. Probably a no-no around here, but desperate times called for desperate measures. After all, he was just their uncle and he was only there for a week, so…

After the popcorn came pizza that he'd heated in the oven. But as the video played it turned out the fantasy wasn't nearly as interesting as the reality of watching Snow White sleep. One by one, the kids crept back into the living room, sat on the carpet and stared at her. Zach opened his mouth to order them out of the room, but they were so quiet and so determined to be involved, he didn't have the heart to banish them.

From Snow White's even breathing, warm skin and flushed face, he deduced she was okay, just tired from her walk and God knew what else she'd been through. How far had she walked? Where was her car? Those questions would have to wait until she came to. In the meantime, he called the nurse to report on Snow White's progress. She told him he'd done all the right things, and to call back if she didn't wake up within the hour.

At eight o'clock, he had to use maximum persuasion to get the kids to bed. He coaxed them up the stairs, one by one, first Millie, then Lily, then Jack and Michael together, one over each shoulder, followed by Brendan and finally Jenny and Mary Ann. Both the girls' and the boys' rooms were dorm-style, with bunk beds and colorful murals painted on the walls by his sister-in-law.

He flicked the boys' light switch. "Good night, Brendan, Michael, Jack," he said.

"'Night, Uncle Zach," they chorused from under their matching comforters with animals marching across the fabric. "Will you come and get us if she wakes up?" Brendan asked.

"Tomorrow. You can see her tomorrow," he said firmly.

Then he went to the girls' room. They peeked up at him from under their pink-and-white comforters.

"Is she really Snow White?" Jenny asked, her blue eyes wide with hope.

"Snow White is just a story," Lily said.

"Just to be sure, you can ask her yourself tomorrow," Zach said.

"I think it's really her, because thee's tho beautiful," Mary Ann said, lisping through her missing front teeth. He only hoped she didn't lose another one or he'd have to play tooth fairy besides everything else.

"Don't you think so, Uncle Zach?"

"Beautiful? Yeah, she's beautiful," he said. "Good night, girls." He closed the door and leaned against it for a minute. Another day down without any major problem—unless you considered the arrival of a half-frozen damsel in distress a major problem. Not that he thought he'd seen the last of the kids for the night. He'd learned the hard way they were likely to need a drink of water or a stuffed animal—or anything to postpone the inevitable final bedtime. But he could always hope. And if he raced downstairs to his laptop computer, he might actually be able to get some work done.

Instead, he found himself sitting across the room, chin resting on his palm, staring at the woman on the couch, admittedly just as fascinated as the kids were. She looked better, he thought. Her hair had dried and curled in soft tendrils around her face. Her cheeks were a healthy pink color, and she appeared to be sleeping soundly, even with a little smile on her lips. She had to be on the road to recovery. And he had to be there when she woke up. To make sure she was really okay. And if she was, he had quite a few questions for the beautiful Snow White.

Beautiful? Oh, yes, she was beautiful. Was she Snow White? No. Was she trouble? Definitely.

Chapter Three

Sabrina opened her eyes slowly and looked around the room. Wood-paneled walls, scuffed hardwood floor, oval braided rug, large, well-worn chairs, mismatched lamps. She was somewhere she'd never been before, and she had no idea how she'd gotten here. All she knew was that she was deliciously warm and dry, which felt heavenly.

Heaven. Now she remembered. She'd died and gone to heaven. Memories nudged their way into her consciousness. A long walk in the snow. A house in the woods. Little faces at the door. A gorgeous man. Then everything had gone black.

Her eyes scanned the room until she saw him, the man, watching her with dark, smoldering eyes and a forehead furrowed with worry lines. Startled, she sat up quickly and the blanket fell to her lap. She looked down to see she was wearing only her underwear. Where was her dress? She grabbed the blanket and wrapped it around her. But not before he'd had a good look at her half-naked breasts. She could tell by the way his mouth twitched and his gaze widened.

"Can I ask you something?" she said. "Are you real or am I dreaming?"

The man grinned. "I'm real. What about you?"

The look he gave her made her flush. Even though she'd been engaged for six months, she was not unaware of the way other men looked at her. But she certainly hadn't checked out any good-looking men. Yet here she was, a stranger in a strange house—half-dressed, no less—and she was boldly looking a man over and liking what she saw.

She liked it so much her heart started thumping madly. As if he were an available male. As if *she* were an available female. Which she wasn't. Or was she?

She thought about Adam. What had happened

when he finally got to the church to find she was gone? Was he suffering? Was he worried about her? She should call and let him know she was okay.

She wondered if he'd simply shrugged and gone back to work. No, he wasn't that heartless. He'd said he loved her. She'd told him she loved him. She thought she did, but now she wasn't sure. She wasn't certain of anything, except that she never should have agreed to marry Adam.

A chill ran up her spine. Was that a reaction to the experience she'd just been through or exposure? Or the look in the stranger's eyes? She tugged on the soft blanket, pulling it securely up to her chin.

She noticed the way the man's hair hung across his forehead, the way the corners of his eyes crinkled when he grinned at her, and the way those dark eyes studied her just as she was studying him. He could be a serial killer. If so, she ought to run out of here right now. As if she was in any condition to run anywhere. Besides, it was so cold outside and so warm inside. Although she had no experience with serial killers, the guy just didn't look like one.

"Where am I?" she asked at last, tearing her gaze from his.

"Five miles north of Piney Ridge, California. Where are you supposed to be?"

She choked on a laugh. "You don't want to know."

"Oh, but I do. I want to know that and a lot more. Shouldn't you be calling someone to tell them you're okay?"

"Am I okay?"

"You look okay. Now, I can't say the same for when you dropped in on us."

"I feel okay," she said, suddenly realizing that she felt remarkably well, all things considered. "Thanks to you. Honestly, I couldn't have walked one more step."

She looked around the room again. There was a small bike parked by the front door and a toy box in the corner overflowing with bright plastic objects. "There were kids here, weren't there? Or did I dream them?"

"Those kids are only too real. With any luck we won't see them until morning, though I can't promise anything. You made quite an impression on them."

"The impression was mutual. I mean, how many were there?"

"Seven, last time I counted."

"Seven kids?" Once again, Sabrina felt as if she might faint. She took a deep breath. "Where's their mother?"

"Their mother is taking a break, which she needed badly," he said.

She'd been lusting over a man with seven kids, who was home while his wife was taking a break. What a great guy. "Seven kids," she repeated. "Wow. They must keep you busy."

"That's the understatement of the year. But enough about them. What about you?"

"Me? There's not much to tell. I was on my way to a motel, which is where I should be going right now." That much was true. "I wonder if I could use your phone."

"To call the motel?"

"To call a tow truck. To pull my car out of the ditch so I can go to a motel."

He waved an arm toward the wall phone. "Be my guest."

She wrapped the blanket around her shoulders and rose to her feet. In the next instant her knees buckled and the man jumped up to catch her in his arms. She stayed there, locked in those warm, strong arms just because it felt so good to be held, to be safe.

"I guess I got up a little too soon," she said breathlessly.

"Wouldn't want you to faint on me again." His lips brushed against her ear. He held her tighter. "Tell me," he said. "How far did you walk in the snow?"

"Too far," she said and reluctantly pulled herself from his arms. "I mean, I really don't know."

"You'd better sit down. Stay here and I'll call the garage for you." He picked up a sweater and drawstring sweatpants from a chair and handed them to her. "Here're some warm clothes. They won't fit, but they might be more comfortable than the dress you came in." Then he turned and went to the kitchen.

By the time he returned, she'd hastily dressed in the baggy clothes.

"Not bad," he said, as his gaze traveled slowly up and down her body from the pushed-up sleeves of the sweater to the rolled-up hems of the pants.

Not bad, but not good, either, she thought. She must look as if she were drowning in these big clothes, whosever they were. "They're a little big but fine," she said, wiping her palms against the soft fleece of the pants.

"Later, I'll look around for something smaller," he said. "Doreen must be about your size."

Doreen... Must be his wife. "I hope she won't mind."

"She won't mind. She owes me big-time. Left me here with her kids for a week."

Sabrina felt a rush of relief mixed with disappointment. "They're not yours?"

"No, thank God."

"What do you mean? From what I saw, I thought they were cute."

"Wait till you get to know them."

"I wish I could, but I really can't stay. What did they say about my car?"

"The tow service is closed for the night. We can try again tomorrow. But the way it's coming down out there, yours won't be the only car in a ditch."

Sabrina looked outside. Even though it was dark, she could see the snow was piled up to the window. "Oh, no."

"Oh, yes. I'm afraid you're stuck here for the night."

Stay overnight with a strange man? And a very attractive one at that? She felt light-headed and hot. It must be the shock. First the icy cold of the outdoors, then the warmth of the house. Why else would she be having these weird symptoms, chills then fever, and hyperawareness of a man she'd never met before.

No, she couldn't stay. What would her parents think? What would Adam say? It didn't matter. She'd left that life behind.

What choice did she have, anyway? Besides, what could happen to her in a house full of kids? Doreen's kids. And who was Doreen? She still didn't know. But she knew the kids weren't his. "I couldn't impose," she said finally.

"Why not? Everyone else has. How do you think I got stuck with this wild bunch? Don't answer that. You look beat. I bet you'd like to use the bathroom and have something to eat." He pointed down the hall. She stood once again and this time didn't falter. Even when she felt his eyes on her the entire way down the hall.

After seeing the bathroom door close, Zach went to the kitchen, opened a can of chunky chicken noodle soup and stared at it absently while he heated it on the stove.

He was filled with relief and curiosity. Relief that she was okay and curiosity about who the hell she was and where she was going. And what was the deal with the wedding dress? He didn't even know her name. All he knew was that she was one gorgeous woman, even half-frozen, half-naked and half-asleep.

Too bad he had to meet her when he was out of his element, babysitting in a remote corner of the state. Otherwise he might have… Might have nothing. He didn't want to start anything with a woman at this point. They always got hysterical or angry when he broke up with them, which he always did eventually.

Even though they seemed self-sufficient, women always wanted more than he was prepared to give. More of his time, more of his energy and more of his attention. They didn't seem to realize he had goals. One of them was to be independent, financially and personally.

Nobody was ever going to come between him and his goals.

"Soup?" he said when she appeared in the kitchen, looking refreshed.

"Yes, please. It smells wonderful." She slid into a seat in the breakfast nook.

He ladled some soup into a bowl and sat down across from her.

"First things first," she said. "Can I use your phone a minute?"

"Sure." So she was finally going to call someone. He could have offered to leave the room after handing her the phone, but he didn't. He was way too curious.

"Hi," she said into the receiver, her eyes on the table. "Just wanted to let you know I'm fine. Don't worry about me. And I'm sorry for what happened. I, uh… I'll explain later." Then she hung up, dialed again two more times and left the same message for two more people. "Message machines," she explained. "Can't live without them."

He nodded. He'd learned nothing. Except that she was sorry and someone—at least three people—might be worried about her. "That's it? Three messages? Nobody else wondering where you are?"

"The word will get around," she said, then dipped into her soup.

He leaned back in his chair and studied her as she ate. Long tapered fingers, polished nails—and a huge diamond on her left hand. She was taken. Before he could ask about the ring, she put her spoon down and asked a question of her own.

"Who's Doreen and how did you get the baby-sitting job?"

"Doreen's my sister-in-law. My brother Al and Doreen are on a minivacation. Their babysitter cancelled at the last minute and they conned me into coming up here for a few days. Now it's my turn."

"To take care of the kids?"

"To ask questions."

She sighed. "Oh."

"Yes, 'oh.' Who are you and what are you doing here?"

"I'm Sabrina White and I'm on vacation."

"In your wedding dress?"

Her cheeks reddened. She didn't deny it. "I didn't have time to change."

"What about your husband? Is he on vacation, too?"

"He doesn't take vacations. And he's not my husband. We didn't get married."

"Last-minute decision?"

"You could say that. Look, I'm extremely grateful to you for taking me in, but…"

"But you want me to butt out of your life."

"I realize that doesn't seem fair, since I've butted into yours."

"I'll make you a deal."

She raised her eyebrows.

"For every question you ask, I get one. Fair?"

"To a certain point. But you owe me," she said. "You've just asked several."

He shrugged. "Go ahead."

"Who are *you?*"

"Zach Prescott." He reached across the table and shook her hand, holding it a little longer than necessary, because it felt so good to hold her soft hand in his. "MBA, Stanford. CEO of Hartley Systems, Palo Alto. Residence, San Francisco. Single, no kids. Anything else?"

Sabrina had a whole list of questions she wanted to ask: Are you a workaholic? Do you like kids? How come a good-looking guy like you is still single? What's wrong with you? There had to be something. But she didn't ask. It was none of her business. She had her own skeletons, after all.

She knew he was a good guy—he was baby-sitting *seven* kids. It was clear he was no serial killer, which was really all she needed to know. Besides, she'd be leaving tomorrow. Then she'd call her parents and Adam again and try to explain.

"Tell me about the kids," she finally said.

"You like kids?"

"Very much. I'm a kindergarten teacher."

"You're kidding. How would you like a job as a nanny for this week?"

She shook her head. "Sorry, I can't. I have to… I have things I've got to do." Return the wedding gifts, apologize to her family and bridesmaids, get the car fixed. The list went on and on. And at the top of the list should be answering the question, why did she run out on her own wedding?

"I see," he said. But she could tell he didn't. "In answer to your question about the kids…what's there to tell? They're basically good kids, but if you're not used to having kids around—and I'm not—they're a handful." He shrugged. "What can I say? I don't know how Al and Doreen manage. But it's what they wanted—a houseful of kids—so that's what they got. These are special children, foster kids, left behind because they're either too old or they've got problems, but Al and Doreen took them in. Al works for the county. Doreen stays home. They don't have much money, but they've made it work. There, that's probably more than you wanted to know."

"No, it's fascinating. They must be amazing people, your brother and his wife."

"No doubt about that. If I didn't know it before, I know it now. I haven't had one minute to myself since they left. I thought I'd be able to get some work done, but…"

"Look, Zach, I'm grateful to you for taking me in and putting me up for the night. I know you need help, but I can't stay here for the week. But maybe I can help you out tomorrow. Give you a break. How would that be? You can even check out my credentials on the web if you want. I'm a kindergarten teacher at Las Lomitas Elementary School. I've been teaching there for seven years."

"Thanks, I appreciate all that. Wow, kindergarten. I guess you're used to an even bigger group of kids."

"Twenty-five," she said.

"What can I say? Maybe it's fate. You need a place to stay, I need some help."

"Just for tomorrow."

"Whatever."

Seven kids? Sabrina had no doubt she could keep them occupied for the day. "What about playing in the snow? I used to love sledding on the hills when I came to the mountains. Have they got sleds? Is there a hill nearby?"

"Yes, yes and yes. All you really have to do is tell them you're Snow White and let them stare at you. But if you want to play with them, too, they'll be ecstatic."

Sabrina smiled. The wedding that never was suddenly seemed ages ago. The soup warmed her insides, and Zach's smile warmed her even more. She was so relaxed her eyelids began drooping.

He must have noticed her fatigue. "Come on upstairs," he said, "I'll show you your room."

"I don't need a room. The couch will be fine."

"No way, Snow White. You deserve a bed of your own. And a prince to wake you up. Isn't that how the story goes?"

"Fairy tales are for kids," she said, suddenly sober. There would be no Prince Charming for her. She wanted too much, way too much. Just ask her stepmother. Just ask Adam.

"Well, these kids are true believers, so anything you can do to play along…"

"I'll do my best. Anyway…" She stood. With an effort. Her knees were weak, and she was so tired she could barely remain upright. But she gave him her best confident smile. "Good night, Zach."

"I'll show you the room."

Zach led the way up the stairs to the master bedroom. He had to suppress his inclination to sweep her up in his arms again and carry her. But she obviously wanted to show him she could stand on her own. So he let her.

When they reached the bedroom, he stood in the doorway for a long moment while she sat on the edge of the bed, a dim bedside lamp the only night. He told himself to leave, go downstairs. She was fine. But he kept picturing her in the middle of that big bed. Kept picturing her in that sexy underwear and imagining how she'd look without it.

"I'm not sure it's my turn," she said, interrupting his thoughts. "But there's something I have to ask."

"Go ahead."

"Who took my dress off?"

He shrugged, a smile lifting one corner of his mouth. She knew damned well who'd taken it off. "Guilty as charged," he said. "But the nurse told me to do it. To prevent hypothermia. You were cold and soaking wet. So I had to take it off, for your own sake, to prevent you from coming down with something serious. You didn't want to get sick, did you?"

"No, I just wondered."

"If it makes you feel any better, I didn't look."

It was her turn to smile. Even in the semidarkness, he saw her lips curve. She was a beauty, no doubt about that. Who was the man she hadn't married? Was he drowning his sorrows tonight, or had *he* left *her?* She didn't seem heartbroken, but what did he know about it? He'd tried hard not to break anyone's heart and his had been broken only once, when he was seven years old. Since then, he'd built a wall around it, emotional protection that worked well.

"I'm afraid the dress is ruined," he said. "It's still in the living room."

"I'm afraid I don't care."

"Who was he?"

Her smile faded. "Sorry," she said. "You've run out of questions."

He held his hands up in surrender. "You can't blame me for trying."

"You saved my life today. I don't want you to think I'm not grateful. But let's just acknowledge we're ships passing in the night. No future, no past. Since we'll probably never see each other again—"

"You'll entertain the kids tomorrow, I'll feel repaid, and then we'll each go our own way."

She shot him a grateful look. "Exactly."

With that, he said good-night and left the room, when what he really wanted to do was sit on the edge of the bed with her and talk. It must be staying here with the kids these past few days that had made him so eager for her companionship. Or maybe it was just that she'd piqued his curiosity. The problem was, the more she told him, the more he wanted to know.

Chapter Four

Sabrina awoke for the second time to unfamiliar surroundings—and to the sight of seven faces peering through the open door of the bedroom. She raised her head, blinked sleepily and that was all it took. The kids burst into the room like a noisy tidal wave, laughing and talking and crowding the edge of the bed, each trying to be closest to her.

Zach appeared next, looking even better than she remembered. He was so ruggedly handsome with his dark hair, dark eyes and the shadow of a beard along his jaw, she couldn't stop staring. He wore a gray sweatshirt, his long legs in jeans. He seemed to fill the room with his ultramasculine presence, while she shivered in the huge sweater he'd loaned her.

She knew it was none of her business, but she couldn't help wondering if he was involved with anyone, or if, by any chance, he was a workaholic. What did it matter? She was in no position to get involved with another man. Besides, if she started asking personal questions, he'd have the right to come back at her with all those questions she didn't want to answer.

He told her that he'd called the garage again and they'd promised to dig her car out sometime today. Then he introduced her bedside guests, one by one, before trying to shoo them out of the room. But they protested vigorously.

"We won't bother her," Lily promised. "Cross my heart."

"We'll be good," Brendan said.

"Please," little blond-haired Millie begged.

Sabrina wanted to hug them all, they were so cute. She told Zach to let them stay and assured him she didn't mind at all.

What she did mind was that she must look like a wreck. She ran a hand self-consciously through her tangled hair. She'd just been thinking how handsome he was, but what must he think of *her?*

Lily brought her a pair of stretch pants and turtlenecked T-shirt from her mother's closet.

"Are you sure your mom won't mind?" Sabrina asked.

Lily shook her head solemnly. "She'd want Snow White to wear her clothes. Unless you've got another white dress?" she asked hopefully.

"Sorry," Sabrina said. "I'm afraid that was my one and only and it's apparently ruined."

She gratefully accepted the clothes, and told the children she'd join them at the breakfast table after she got dressed.

By the time she arrived in the kitchen the kids were too excited to eat much of anything, but Sabrina found she was hungry, happily accepting a piece of toast Zach offered her.

"Feeling okay?" he asked, as he filled her coffee cup.

"Just fine."

"Sure you want to go outside with the kids?"

"Of course. What about you?"

He hesitated and she thought he'd decline. She couldn't imagine Adam taking time to play in the snow. Maybe Zach didn't have a very demanding job. But that didn't seem likely. He was a CEO.

Zach reached for his jacket. "Fresh snow, sunshine. How can I resist?"

Adam would have resisted. He would have told her it was kid stuff, playing in the snow. Why had it taken her so long to realize how little they really had in common? Probably because everyone around her, especially her family, kept telling her how much they had in common. On the surface, yes. They'd gone to the same schools and had mutual friends. But somewhere along the line they'd both changed. Sabrina had become a teacher, with long vacations. Adam had gone into business and took no vacations. Not even weekends off. So even though they were engaged to be married, they'd drifted apart, each immersed in their separate lives.

She didn't want to think about Adam right now. She'd told Zach she would help him. So she joined him in getting the kids dressed to go outside. Once they'd accomplished that, he gave her his sister-in-law's outerwear—jacket, scarf, gloves and boots—and, together, they went to the garage to collect the sleds, inflatable tubes and toboggan and headed for the nearest hill.

"I thought I was going to give you a break," Sabrina said, feeling energized by the bracing cold air as they walked along the snowy road.

"This *is* a break," he said. "Why should you have all the fun?"

She smiled. He smiled back, a killer smile that sent a wave of heat through her body that had nothing to do with the down jacket he'd loaned her. How come this man had not been snapped up by now? He was good-looking. Too good to be true.

Maybe he'd come along this morning just for the adult company after being trapped with the kids for three days. Whatever his reason, she was glad he'd come along.

The kids, she quickly realized, were hard to keep track of. Not at all like her class when they were out in the schoolyard at recess. They yelled at one another, threw snowballs, and chased one another in the snow-laden pine trees.

When they reached the hill, Sabrina organized the children's runs. She took the two smallest girls, Jenny and Millie, on the toboggan with her, wrapping her arms around them, hugging them tightly. Zach gave them a push and they flew downhill, stopping abruptly in front of a snowbank. A few minutes later, Zach and Michael came rushing past them on a sled.

Michael was screaming with delight as they plowed into the snowbank. Zach picked him up and brushed him off, his cheeks as red as the kids'. He looked so virile and at home in the outdoors, she grinned at him from where she sat on the toboggan.

"Having fun?" he asked.

"Great. I feel like a kid again, don't you?"

"Lord, no. Why would I want to feel like a kid again?"

"Because childhood has got to be the happiest, the most carefree time of your life. Even though my mom died when I was young, I still have a lot of wonderful memories."

"Carefree and happy does not exactly describe my childhood," he said with a frown.

Surprised by this abrupt disclosure, Sabrina gave him a sympathetic look. "I'm sorry to hear that," she said softly.

"Don't worry about it," he said, his voice even and his frown gone. "I don't. It was a long time ago and I got over it."

"Yes, but…"

"Speaking of getting over it, you're a very resilient person, Ms. White. Yesterday you were out of it, to say the least. Today, look at you." He looked at her, in a way that made her heart skip a beat. "What's your secret?"

"Not sure I've got one." *Resilient?* She hoped so. She'd need resilience to bounce back from her aborted wedding. So would Adam. "Are you sure you don't want to go back to the house to get your work done?"

"And leave you alone with this wild bunch?" he teased.

She suddenly wondered if he was afraid to trust her alone with the kids. She didn't blame him. He didn't know her. He was responsible for these children. If he hadn't checked her credentials online, for all he knew, *she* was the serial killer.

He held out a gloved hand to help Sabrina up. That simple touch caused her knees to shake. The man had a very strange effect on her and she didn't understand it. Unless it was the altitude.

Yesterday, she'd almost married another man; today, she was giddy from a stranger's touch. It would be a long time before she trusted her instincts or her judgment again. She'd escaped one disastrous mistake. If she'd learned anything, it was not to rush into a new relationship.

"Uncle Zach," Brendan called from the top of the hill. "My turn."

"No, mine," Jack yelled.

"Gotta go," Zach said and trudged back up the hill, pulling the sled and holding Michael's hand.

After a morning of sledding, they returned to the house for lunch, which was more canned soup.

Sabrina looked around the table at the ruddy-faced children. Michael spilled his milk. Brendan poked Jenny in the ribs, and she poked him back. Millie said she hated the soup. They called one another names.

"Dopey."

"Stinky."

"Cuckoo-head."

"Sneezy."

"Grumpy."

Sabrina sighed, but had to admit she'd heard worse on the schoolyard. It would take more than name-calling to discourage her from wanting a houseful of kids of her own, though. She knew such a life wouldn't be all fun and games, but at that moment, feeling the glow of a morning of exercise in the fresh, cold mountain air, watching the faces around the table, listening to them talk and argue and tease one another, she had a vision of what it could be like. A little of the unexpected. A little chaos now and then. A *lot* of smiles and togetherness.

That had not been her childhood. She'd had organized fun, lessons, trips and vacations, but spent a lot of time alone. She wanted to bring up a child differently, with siblings and two committed parents. That was what Adam had pretended to want, too, but how would he ever make time for kids when he couldn't seem to make time for *her?*

The garage called with a report on the car as she and Zach were stacking the lunch dishes in the sink. The mechanic told her they were going to straighten the fender and put a new tire on the car and that she could pick it up the *next* morning. That meant staying the rest of the day—and another night—in this house. If that was okay with Zach.

He nodded.

"Is that really okay?" she asked after she hung up. He'd said okay, but was he sorry, surprised or worried that she was staying another night? She certainly didn't want to overstay her welcome.

"Of course. I just wish…"

Sabrina never knew what he was going to say

because just then Mary Ann burst into tears because someone had taken her cracker.

Later in the afternoon they took the kids back out to the hill. While the kids watched and cheered, Sabrina and Zach rode the toboggan downhill, Sabrina sitting behind Zach, her arms wrapped tightly around his waist.

Halfway down the toboggan hit an icy patch, tipped over and Sabrina found herself on top of Zach, her face only inches from his. Laughing, he rolled them over, until he was on top of her.

"You're really enjoying this, aren't you?" he said.

"Aren't you?" she asked.

His mouth was so close to hers, she thought he was going to kiss her. Of course he didn't. There were seven kids watching them. But she couldn't help thinking that *if* he'd kissed her, she'd have kissed him back.

"I can't believe this," she said, putting her hands on his shoulders to create some distance. "Yesterday I was…in a different place."

"And tomorrow? Do you really have to leave tomorrow?"

"Yes." Tomorrow she'd have to face her very real problems.

He nodded and stood, once again pulling her

up out of the snow. The sun was setting behind the mountains when the began the walk back to the house, the snow crunching under their feet. Zach and Sabrina held hands with Brendan and Mary Ann while the older kids held the little ones' hands. It was like a scene from *The Sound of Music,* Sabrina thought.

Memories of childhood trips to these mountains came back to her again. If only she'd had six brothers and sisters to keep her company, instead of being left at ski school by her stepmother who went off to ski with her friends. How different her childhood would have been.

"Are you telling me you and your brother didn't have fun like this when you were kids?" Sabrina asked Zach.

"Hah," he said. "Not likely. I never saw snow until I was nineteen."

"Still, you were lucky you weren't an only child. At least you weren't lonely."

He shot her a look that told her she didn't know what she was talking about. But he didn't elaborate. So she was left to wonder, what kind of a childhood had he had?

Based on his silence the remainder of the walk home, she wouldn't know anytime soon.

After a dinner of spaghetti and tomato sauce, which had been in the freezer, packaged and labeled, Sabrina sat down to read the kids a story. The girls demanded *Snow White,* the boys wanted *Spider-Man.* To put an end to their argument, she read both.

"Sabrina," Lily said, the picture book *Snow White* in one hand, her other hand clutching Sabrina's arm, "when you get married to the prince, can we be in your wedding?"

The other children nodded vigorously.

"Please," they said.

"Can we?"

"We'll be good."

"Say yes!"

Sabrina couldn't say no. So she said yes. She didn't want to explain that the chances of her getting married, let alone to a prince, were almost zero.

They were so excited that they chattered like little magpies and she thought they'd never fall asleep. Finally she got them into their beds, turned the lights off and went downstairs.

When Sabrina walked into the living room, tired but keyed up at the same time, feeling just a little guilty for promising the kids something she didn't think she could deliver, she saw that Zach had made a fire in the hearth. And he was standing in the middle of the room staring into the flames.

"They're all in bed," she said.

The scene was too perfect. Kids all tucked into their beds and a man waiting in front of a blazing fire. Yesterday, she'd been a runaway bride; today, she'd fallen into a fairy-tale scenario. One that she'd only dreamed about. But it wasn't real. The kids belonged to someone else, and for all she knew, so did the man.

She sat on the couch and tucked her legs under her.

Zach turned his head in her direction. "I don't know how to thank you."

"What for? I was supposed to give you a day off, but you didn't take it."

"Yes, I did. I had a good time today," he said soberly.

"You sound surprised."

"I am. If you'd told me yesterday I'd be playing in the snow today, I would have said you were crazy."

"Same here. I didn't expect this. I told you, I felt like a kid again."

"You acted like one of them," he said with a grin.

"They're wonderful kids. I know they fight and argue, but you can tell they care about each other. I love the way Lily looks after the little ones. And the way Jack and Michael tease each other. I know they're lucky to be here, but your brother and his wife are very lucky, too."

Zach nodded. "I know they are, but before you came I felt like I was swimming upstream, battling for control every minute. Wishing they'd settle down, wishing they'd sit quietly and stop bothering me. Wishing I could ignore them and get my work done. In other words, wishing they weren't kids. Well, today you gave me the chance to work. And what did I do?"

"You played hooky."

He nodded slowly. "And tomorrow you'll be on your way."

"You'll be fine. The kids adore you, I can see that." It was true. They loved their Uncle Zach. And he loved them. He just didn't admit it. At least, not to her.

"They have a strange way of showing it," he said. "Before you came, they protested everything I told them to do."

"They were probably testing you to see how much they could get away with."

"I don't blame them," he said, turning off the lights so the room was illuminated only by the flickering flames from the fireplace.

He sat next to her on the couch, his hip pressed against hers. She wanted his arms around her, his mouth on hers. She wanted to put her arms around him and feel his heart beat in time with hers. She told herself she was on the rebound. It didn't take a genius to recognize that. Yet, armed with that knowledge, she was powerless to stop what was happening between them.

He framed her face with his hands and looked deep into her eyes. "Because I've been wondering the same thing. How much can I get away with?"

"How much do you want to get away with?" she murmured.

He kissed her, and she wrapped her arms around his neck and kissed him back. Yes, this was what she wanted. This was what she needed. Her pulse raced. She felt his heart beat through his sweatshirt. Or was that hers? She couldn't tell.

"I want to get away with this," he muttered, kissing the hollow of her throat. "And this," he said, trailing kisses along the curve of her cheek.

She giggled, then slid her hands under his

sweatshirt to feel his chest. His skin was warm to the touch, the muscles firm and sculpted. The laughter died in her throat and she was left breathless.

Zach growled in the back of his throat. He wanted her. He'd wanted her since she first appeared at his door—had it been only last night? He knew quite a bit about her now. According to her school's Web site, she'd been named Teacher of the Year—something she was too modest to tell him. She was *not* married, was great with kids… and she was running away from something.

All day he'd been thinking about getting her alone. Especially after that missed opportunity to kiss her in the snow. He wanted her warm and naked, but that wasn't going to happen. She'd almost married someone else yesterday. Just when he was thinking he couldn't take advantage of her or the situation, she looked at him with half-closed eyes and said breathlessly, "Kiss me again."

He didn't need a second invitation. His whole body was on fire. The touch of her hands on his chest had started the flames and now he couldn't put them out if he tried.

He kissed her again and again, harder and harder, moving his lips over hers until they parted and her tongue met his in a dance as old as time. She shivered, and he pulled a throw over her shoulders without missing a beat.

How they landed on the floor he never knew. But they'd rolled in front of the fire, still locked in each other's arms.

She was on top of him and her silky hair brushed against his cheek. "It's déjà vu all over again," she said lightly, her eyes burning as brightly as the flames.

"Warm down here," he said, yanking his sweatshirt off with one hand, the other on the small of her back to keep her right where she was.

She nodded and took off her shirt, too, one sleeve at a time, revealing her lace demibra.

Sabrina felt feverish and yet her skin was covered with goose bumps. In all the time she'd been with Adam, she'd never felt this way. Why? She'd been in love with Adam, hadn't she? Or had she just *wanted* to be in love with him because everyone said they were so right together?

Did she feel more passion with Zach because he was a ship in the night, never to be seen again after tomorrow? Was she just a thrill-seeker, or was she a frustrated runaway bride suffering from an overdose of forbidden lust?

Whatever the reason, she didn't want this moment to stop. Every beat of her heart made her want him more.

"You're on fire," she said, running her hand across the warm skin of his smooth shoulder.

"You've got that right," he said, shifting his weight to look down at her with coal-hot eyes. Her breath seemed to catch in her throat.

The front door opened, a shaft of cold air blew across her heated body and a man's voice broke the silence. "Hello?"

Sabrina's heart thudded wildly. Good heavens, who was he and what was he doing here?

Zach got to his knees and offered her his hand. But she ignored him, grabbed her shirt and thrust her arms in the sleeves.

"Al," Zach said, "what are you doing back so soon?"

"Came back early because Doreen was worried about the kids," he said. "By the way, what are *you* doing? And who's the lady?"

Chapter Five

"Sabrina White, this my brother Al and his wife, Doreen," Zach said, his voice rough and uneven.

Sabrina got to her feet, as gracefully as she could with her hair probably a mess and her clothes wrinkled. Correction, clothes belonging to the woman standing in front of her, gazing at her with some surprise. Who could blame her?

"I, uh…I'm happy to meet you," Sabrina said, breathing hard.

"Sabrina's a friend of mine," Zach said. "Dropped in as a surprise to see how I was doing. Believe me, she's been a big help."

"How nice of her," Doreen enthused with a big smile. "I wish we'd known you were coming."

"So do I." Zach gave her a pointed look that made her blush.

"How are the kids?" Al asked.

"Sound asleep," Zach said. "We wore them out today playing in the snow."

"You look worn out yourself," Al said, hitting his brother playfully on the shoulder. "Lost your shirt?"

"Oh, that. It's around here somewhere."

Zach didn't seem that bothered to be caught on the floor of his brother's living room half-dressed and cavorting with a strange woman. But for all Sabrina knew, that was what he always did when babysitting.

"I'm going upstairs to check on the kids," Doreen said after a long, searching look at her brother-in-law. Al asked Zach to join him in the kitchen to make coffee. Sabrina found herself suddenly alone.

"So who is this woman?" Al asked in a loud whisper as he measured the coffee grounds.

"I told you," Zach said. "Her name is—"

"I know what her name is. I don't know *who*

she is. You've never brought anyone up here before. You've never even introduced us to anyone before. She must be pretty special." Al nudged him in the ribs.

Zach frowned. Oh, great, now his brother would be on his case forever. For weeks, months, maybe years, he'd be asking about the mysterious Sabrina White. Long after she had gone back to where she came from.

"She's not special, she's just…a friend."

"Looked like a very good friend from what I saw." His brother chuckled.

"Okay, a very good friend. But don't get any ideas."

"Who *me*? Get ideas?" Al asked. "Ideas about you and some woman? I know better than that. But that doesn't stop me from hoping someday you'll change your mind. Find someone to love and settle down."

"It's not going to happen," Zach said as firmly as he could. How many times did he have to repeat his mantra? No wife, no kids, no house with a picket fence around it. "By the way, I *am* settled down. Just not the way you want."

"I know my lifestyle is not something you want," Al said. "But that doesn't mean—"

"I like my life the way it is. It's not something that just happened because I haven't found Ms. Right, because there is no such person. It's my choice. Especially after all we went through as kids. I guess an analyst would say we have different ways of dealing with our past. I respect your way, so why can't you respect mine?"

Al held out his hands palm forward. "Okay, okay, I respect it. I won't say another word. I won't ask about Ms. White out there. I won't tell you she doesn't look like your usual type—though I can see she's one gorgeous girl. And I won't ask what you two were up to on the floor in there because I think I know. So go back to the city, get back to your job that takes up all your time and enjoy life. You *do* enjoy life, don't you?"

"Of course I do," Zach said, with more emphasis than absolutely necessary.

He shouldn't have to explain to Al, of all people, that he enjoyed knowing that *he* was in control of his life. Not an institution, not some faceless state bureaucracy, and not someone who was getting paid for taking him in. Definitely not some woman. Just himself.

Maybe Al didn't understand because he was the little brother, the cute little kid everyone always loved, whereas Zach, as the older sibling, had been responsible for them both, and full of pent-up anger for the people who'd left the two of them behind.

In the living room Sabrina sat on the couch, waiting for someone, anyone, and trying to think of where to go and how to leave gracefully.

When Doreen finally joined her after checking on her children, she said, "They're great kids," hoping to head off any embarrassing questions, such as, how did you meet Zach? And why haven't we heard him mention you before?

"Yes, they are." Doreen beamed proudly. "But they can be a handful. It was good of you to come up here and help Zach out. If I'd known…"

"I really didn't know myself until the last minute," Sabrina said. "Which is why I'm wearing your clothes. I didn't know I'd be staying."

"I'm delighted they fit," Doreen said. "I hope you won't rush off, now that we're home. Maybe we can persuade you and Zach to hang around for a few days for some fun in the snow? I think he needs a break."

"I think you're right," Sabrina said. "But I

really have to leave. In fact, I can't impose on you another minute. I'm going to call a taxi and—"

"A taxi? At this time of night? I'm afraid you'd be out of luck. If you don't mind the couch, we'd love to have you stay."

"You're very kind to offer. The truth is, I want to see the kids again before I leave to say goodbye. They're so cute, and I got kind of attached to them."

"You don't have any of your own, I take it," Doreen said.

"No, I don't. But hopefully someday."

"Well, Zach is a great guy," Doreen said. "He just needs the right woman to help him settle down. Get over the past. I'm hoping maybe you and he…"

Sabrina bit her lip. "Uh, no, not really." She shifted on the couch, wanting badly to know what Doreen meant about Zach 'getting over the past,' but not wanting to mislead her into thinking they were serious about each other. It was understandable they'd gotten that impression after catching her and Zach rolling around on the floor.

"You'd never know they were brothers," Doreen continued as if Sabrina hadn't corrected her misconception. "They're so different."

Sabrina was hoping Doreen would elaborate on her statement about the brothers' differences, maybe reveal something about Zach's past, but the men came back into the living room with four coffee mugs on a tray before she could say anything.

"Kids okay?" Al asked his wife.

"Sound asleep," Doreen reported, handing Sabrina her coffee. "Except for Lily who said Snow White had come here. What an imagination. You must have tired them out, Zach."

"They tired *me* out, is more like it. Up and down the hill about one hundred times, right, Sabrina?"

"It was fun," Sabrina said. "I felt young again."

"How can we ever thank you?" Doreen asked, looking at Zach, then Sabrina.

"I'll think of something," Zach said, stirring his coffee.

"Can you stay another day, Zach?" Doreen asked. "Give us a chance to get caught up."

"Sorry, but now that you're home, I've got some things to do in the city."

"Then you'll be driving back together?" Al asked, with a sideways glance at his brother.

"No," Sabrina said. "My car was slightly

damaged when it went off the road yesterday, but it's supposed to be ready tomorrow for me to drive myself home."

"Then the two of you will caravan?" Doreen asked.

Sabrina looked at Zach, who shrugged at her. No, the best thing to do was to take off first thing in the morning—by herself—and drive as fast as possible back to the city where she would try to mollify her parents, and try to explain to Adam why she'd run.

How badly had she hurt him? Would he forgive her? Would he understand what had made her do it? She shuddered, thinking of the look on his face when he arrived at the church to find her gone.

Mistaking her shudder for a chill, Zach retrieved the afghan from the floor and wrapped it around her shoulders. The touch of his hands made her instantly burn up again. She noticed Al and Doreen exchanging glances. They must be wondering what was going on between them. Who could blame them? She was wondering herself.

They never answered Doreen's question, talking instead about the weather, the kids and winter sports. Finally, Doreen and Al said goodnight. Zach retreated to a foam pad in the laundry room. And Sabrina curled up on the couch with a pillow and the blanket she'd used the previous night.

She lay there, staring at the ceiling, her mind spinning. What would have happened if Doreen and Al hadn't arrived home when they did? She wanted to think that common sense would have prevailed. That she would have sat up, dusted herself off and said, "Let's be sensible. Considering I was about to marry someone else yesterday, I'm in no position to get into a new relationship." But then he might have said, "Chill out. Who's getting into a new relationship? All I want is a good time."

She sighed, turned over and buried her flushed face in the pillow. What must they think of her? More importantly, what must Zach think of her?

In the morning, after a night of tossing and turning until she had finally fallen into a restless sleep, Sabrina awoke to the children begging her to stay. She hugged them each, one at a time, and promised she'd write them a letter. She actually felt teary-eyed when she finally walked out the front door wearing Doreen's pants, shirt, jacket and boots.

"I'll send the clothes back," she promised.

"Even better, bring them back in person," Doreen said.

Sabrina smiled, but swallowed hard to keep from crying. She knew she wouldn't be back. These were special people, this was a unique family, but they weren't *her* family. She had a lot of fence-mending to do with her family.

She hurried to Zach's car. He'd offered to drop her at the garage and then be on his way.

"You're crying?" he asked, sending a sideways glance in her direction once they were headed down the mountain.

She wiped her eyes. "It's the kids. They really got to me. They're so sweet."

"They really liked you."

"You, too."

"I guess they do."

"Thanks for sharing your family with me. They're really wonderful people."

"You're welcome," Zach said.

They drove in silence the rest of the way to Piney Ridge. Finally Zach pulled over and parked. "Well, here's the garage."

"There's my car. Actually, my friend's car. It looks like new, thank God."

"I'll wait here to make sure everything's okay."

Sabrina slid out of the passenger seat. She didn't want any awkward goodbyes. No farewell kisses or promises to keep in touch when they both knew they weren't going to.

"Ships that pass in the night," he said before she closed the door. "Right?"

She nodded. "Right."

But when she came out of the garage, waved to him with the keys in her hand, then watched him pull away, her eyes filled with tears again before spilling down her cheeks. What was wrong with her? There was nothing to be sad about. She'd met seven cute children. Two remarkable parents.

And one unforgettable man.

She was lucky. She'd glimpsed the kind of life-style she wanted. *If* she ever found a man who wanted the same. And she knew now, with absolute certainty, that Adam wasn't that man.

She should be thankful for the clarity. Still, she grieved for what was lost. The fairy tale.

But there was no sense crying like a baby about it. So, brushing away her tears, she started the car and headed back to real life. Hours later she remembered she'd left her wedding dress behind. It didn't matter. She wouldn't be needing it.

Chapter Six

"I'm sorry about your car," Sabrina said to Meg, as she handed her best friend a cup of peach-flavored tea.

"The car's fine. But what about you?"

"I'm fine, too."

"Tell me where you went and what you did," Meg demanded, ensconced in one of the over-stuffed chair in Sabrina's pale-peach-and-green living room.

"I stayed with a family up in the mountains after getting stuck. Once I got your car towed and repaired, I came back. End of story."

"End of story? I don't believe you. You've been back for a week now, but you're not really here."

"Of course I'm here. Where else would I be?" Sabrina said. But she knew where she was. She was in the mountains in the snow with seven kids and a sexy stranger.

"You're somewhere else. You don't always answer when spoken to, and you've got a faraway look in your eyes."

Sabrina laughed self-consciously. She thought she'd have forgotten Zach by now, but she hadn't. In fact, she couldn't stop thinking about him.

"This is an awkward time," Sabrina said. "I walked out on my wedding. Why? Because I knew it was the right thing to do. Adam has been very understanding, for someone who was humiliated, as he says. He did have to explain to the guests there'd be no wedding."

"*He* was humiliated?" Meg said indignantly. "What about you? What about keeping you waiting at the church for half an hour? He didn't even arrive for another half hour. Maybe you're being a little too easy on him."

"I don't know about that. I still feel guilty, even though he seems to have fully recuperated and retreated back into his work, almost as if nothing happened. He thinks—and Genevieve and my father think—that I had a bad case of wedding jitters and pretty soon I'll be back to my old self. Maybe even decide to reschedule the wedding, if you can believe that."

"What do you think?" Meg asked, sipping her tea.

Sabrina shook her head. "I did the right thing. And I have no intention of changing my mind."

"You'll find someone else."

"In a few years, after I recover, maybe. I don't trust my judgment anymore. Not after this. I've hurt Adam, and I've hurt my parents. No, I don't think I'll be ready to get married again anytime soon. To anyone."

"How's school been?"

"I'm glad to be back in the classroom. The kids thought I was getting married, so I had to explain my name hadn't changed after all. I don't know what I'd do without my precious kindergartners. Especially since I won't be having any kids of my own."

"Sabrina, don't be too sure. I can't picture you as a withered-up spinster."

"Thanks, Meg. My stepmother hasn't given up on a wedding, either. She feels cheated. To make matters worse, she wants me back out on the social scene. The last place I want to be. Did you know the Apple Charity Ball is coming up next Saturday? She's bought tickets, and she and my dad are insisting that I go. It makes me cringe to think of it. Facing everyone."

"Oh, you have to go. I'm going. It's for a good cause. The children's hospital. Oh, and there's going to be an auction of eligible bachelors."

"You're going to bid on a date?" Sabrina asked, wide-eyed. "You would do that in front of the whole world? Oh, wait a minute. Your old flame, Granger, wouldn't be one of the eligible bachelors, would he?"

Meg set her teacup down, stood and paced in front of one of the bay windows. "He could be. At least, that's what I heard. But I can't get up and shout out my bid in front of the whole world without some moral support from my best friend. You said you owed me." She turned to face Sabrina. "You said anything, anything at all."

What choice did she have? The annual Apple Charity Ball, attended by the superrich and super-social, was the kind of thing Sabrina hated. But if she went, her parents would be placated and she'd help out her best friend who'd been there for her when she needed her.

She sighed. "It's a deal."

On the big night, ten days later, Meg dressed at Sabrina's apartment. She was glad to have Meg to worry about instead of herself. Would her friend have the nerve to bid on Granger? Would they get back together? Meg was obviously nervous; she tripped over the chair in front of the makeup mirror in Sabrina's bathroom.

Meg stood up, shaky in her push-up bra and sheer stockings. "I can't go. I can't go through with it. You go without me."

Sabrina put an arm around her friend. "We have to go. We have our tickets and my stepmother, for one, will be furious if I don't show. And I'm *not* going by myself."

Meg sat down in front of the mirror and stared at herself, her mouth turned down at the corners.

"I'm not saying we have to stay all night," Sabrina said. "If you don't want to bid on Granger, don't. We'll simply put in an appearance. We'll smile, we'll dance, we'll even flirt. Everyone will think we're having a good time. No one will think you're pining over Granger."

"I'm *not!*"

"I know you're not," Sabrina said soothingly. "I'm just saying no one will think that. Whatever you do, I'm behind you."

Meg stood and hugged Sabrina. "Thanks," she said.

By the time Sabrina zipped up Meg's short, floaty lavender dress, Meg had calmed down. At least on the outside. Meg's breakup with Granger was all due to a silly misunderstanding, and Meg had stubbornly refused to make the first move toward a reconciliation. Tonight was her chance. And Sabrina was determined to get her friend and Granger back together if possible. If she did, she could leave and go home by herself.

"Wow," Meg said, standing back to look at Sabrina when she emerged in a long, form-fitting black halter dress and black strappy sandals. "You look terrific. Who are you trying to impress?"

"Nobody," Sabrina said. "Believe me, I've sworn off men. But I hate to waste the dress I bought for my honeymoon cruise. Where else could I wear it except to a black-tie benefit?"

Sabrina glanced at herself in the mirror. Was the neckline too low? Did the low back leave her too exposed?

"Come on, let's go before I lose *my* nerve," she said. The worst part of this evening was going to be facing people she hadn't seen since her wedding fiasco. Waiting for the questions on everyone's lips.

Where did you go?

Why did you run away?

When is the wedding going to be?

A short time later, the taxi let them off at the Civic Center, where the streets were closed off and huge tents were set up. Searchlights illuminated the night sky, and the historic buildings that framed the square were lighted by spotlights. Inside the tents fragrant blossoming apple trees were everywhere, the apples hanging from the branches gilded with silver. A big band in the center of one of the tents played old favorites.

"It's beautiful," Sabrina said. She'd been determined not to give in to the phony romantic atmosphere, but she couldn't help admire the artistry required to put on a display like this. The lush setting and nostalgic music almost made her wish she were with someone special. The irony that she'd just escaped marrying someone she thought was special, but wasn't, didn't escape her notice. Now if only she could avoid anyone who'd been at her wedding or heard about it.

Fat chance.

Everyone who was anyone was there. Sabrina had just pasted a smile on her face, when she saw him. He was on the other side of the room with a stunning blonde draped on his arm.

The man she'd spent two days with in the mountains.

The man she'd been trying to forget ever since.

Sabrina gasped and stopped abruptly.

"What's wrong?" Meg asked. "You look like you just saw a ghost."

"Not a ghost," Sabrina said. "Just someone I'd rather not see just now. Or, to be more exact, someone I don't want to see me."

But he did see her. At that moment, as if by magic, Zach turned. His gaze met hers and held for a long, long moment. The babble of voices and the music faded away and it was just the two of them, across a great divide and yet together again. The air was sucked clear out of her lungs and she didn't know if she'd ever be able to breathe normally again.

"Whoever he is, he's coming this way," Meg said under her breath. "And he's not taking his time about it."

Sabrina's knees went weak. She couldn't faint. Not again. Not this time. He already thought she was some ditzy female who'd appeared in a wedding dress in the middle of a snowstorm and fainted at his doorstep. She had to show him she was not that woman. But the room was spinning around. She'd thought she'd never see him again. She should have known better. San Francisco was a small town. Getting smaller by the minute.

"Who is he and what does he want with you?" Meg asked urgently. "Did you hear me?" she said, worriedly glancing at Sabrina.

Sabrina nodded.

"Now what?"

"Now nothing," Sabrina said. "I'm fine. Just caught me off guard."

"Who did? The guy who's walking toward us like he's just had a glimpse of the brass ring?" Meg asked.

"Just don't leave me," Sabrina begged.

"Why? Is he dangerous?" Meg asked.

"Dangerous to my peace of mind, that's all," Sabrina muttered.

But that wasn't all. He was dangerous to her resolve to give up on men. He was dangerous to her shaky nerves and her plan to forget about him completely.

"Well, if it isn't Snow White," Zach said with a disarming smile that sent shivers up her bare arms. "What a surprise to see you here."

Sabrina managed a weak smile in return. What was there about a man in a tux? It could turn even an ordinary man into something special, but a hunk like Zach Prescott? Sabrina's mouth was so dry she could barely speak, he was so gorgeous. It was the contrast of the white shirt and his dark hair and eyes.

"Nice to see you again, Zach," she said when she found her voice. "This is my friend, Meg."

"The owner of the Beemer?"

"Yes."

"Now how did you know that?" Meg asked, carefully giving Zach the once-over. "And what's this about Snow White?"

"Nothing," Sabrina said, hoping Zach would catch on that the Snow White episode was in the past and that she'd prefer to forget about it. She'd prefer to forget him, too, but it didn't look as if that was going to happen anytime soon. Just the sight of him and the sound of his voice sent her pulse racing.

"Just a case of mistaken identity," Zach said smoothly. "Seeing you tonight in black, I realize you couldn't possibly be Snow White. On the other hand, you look too good to be real, so maybe you've just stepped out of a different fairy tale." His eyes gleamed, and Sabrina blushed. "Help me out here. Which one could it be?"

"Look, uh…" Sabrina struggled to think of something clever to say.

"Zach. The name is Zach."

"I know who you are."

"You know a lot about me and my relatives, but I don't know much about you and yours."

Sabrina noticed that Meg was turning her head from side to side, her nose wrinkled, watching and listening and wondering what to make of this whole thing. Sabrina didn't blame her for being puzzled. She scarcely knew what to make of it, either.

She gave up on clever and struggled to find something impersonal to say. "How are the kids?" she asked at last.

"Kids?" Meg asked. "You have kids?"

Zach shook his head. "Not me. My brother has exceeded the quota for the family, so I'm off the hook."

"His brother has seven children," Sabrina explained. If she had ever been under the illusion that Zach was planning on being a family man, she had no such illusions any longer. "All adorable," she added.

"I see," Meg said. But Sabrina knew she didn't see, and that she was dying to ask for details, such as who is this guy? Where did you meet him? And why hadn't she heard about him or these adorable kids?

"They asked about you," Zach said.

Sabrina teetered on her high-heeled sandals. "About *me?*" she asked. It touched her more than she'd imagined to know the kids remembered her.

"I talked to them last night. Doreen had your dress cleaned for you. They all hope you'll come to pick it up and play in the snow again."

"I'm feeling more and more out of this conversation," Meg said with a playful nudge at Sabrina. "I see an old friend I should say hello to, if you two will excuse me?"

Sabrina nodded, letting her friend off the hook, but she really wished Meg wouldn't leave her alone with Zach. He had the same effect on her he'd had in the mountains, and this time she couldn't blame it on the altitude. She had to blame it on the chemistry between them. But she was not going to fall for someone because he was a gorgeous guy who was good with kids but didn't want any of his own. She was not going to fall for anyone at all until she recovered from her near-wedding to the wrong man, and fully recovered her wits. She would never again be unduly influenced by her family. In the meantime, she made a note to stay away from social functions like this one.

"How've you been?" he asked. It struck a chord somewhere around her heart.

She swallowed hard. "Fine, just fine. I'm back at school and everything's fine. What about you? Are you caught up with your work?"

Zach nodded. He would never be caught up with his work. That was the kind of job he had. But suddenly he couldn't remember a single detail of the project he was working on. All he knew was that he'd promised months ago to be on hand for this charity auction, but he had never expected to see Sabrina here. He had never expected to see her ever again, though he'd been thinking about her, reliving the few days they'd had together, from the moment she'd tumbled into the house until their goodbye.

He knew it was for the best that they'd parted, because he had a gut feeling she was the kind of woman he just might fall for and shouldn't. But there had been times during the past two weeks when he'd actually thought about looking her up.

Now, seeing her up close in that sexy dress, he was overcome with urges he didn't know how to handle. The urge to kiss her, to see her again, to find out more about her. The one urge he gave in to was to reach up into the apple tree above their heads and tear off a blossom. He leaned forward and put it behind her ear.

He smiled with satisfaction. "Looks good on you."

She blushed. "Smells good. I can't believe they're real."

"That's how I feel about you. Can't believe you're real."

She reached up, plucked a blossom and stuck it in his buttonhole. "Now we're even," she said, her smile matching his.

"Not by a long shot," he said. He knew he shouldn't flirt with Sabrina. It was like flirting with danger. She was not his type. She wanted a life like his brother's. She'd made that clear. Not to mention, she had secrets.

What had happened to her groom? Had they gotten back together? If they had, the guy was a fool for letting her out of his sight, looking as sexy as she did in that black dress. But she appeared to be dateless. And if she was, what was he going to do about it?

"I think your date is looking for you," she said, with a nod toward the blonde he'd been talking to.

"I don't have a date," he said. "I'm only here for the auction."

"You're auctioning yourself off?" she asked incredulously.

"I got roped into it. It's for charity, you know."

"I know, that's why I'm here."

"Then I hope you'll bid on me," he said with a grin.

"I can't do that. I only came because Meg wants to bid on one of the guys."

"If you bid on me, I won't have to go out with someone I don't know. Imagine spending a weekend with a complete stranger." But the minute he said the words, he thought about his time with Sabrina. The thought made his heart pound.

"A weekend? I thought it was just a date," Sabrina said.

"Too much time to spend with me, huh? I understand," he teased. He did understand. She'd already spent quite a lot of time with him. The problem was, he hadn't spent enough time with her.

"They upped the prize to make more money," Zach explained. "They kicked in a getaway weekend at some hotels, dinner at some restaurants, etc., etc. All donated. You know how these things go."

"Well, hello, Sabrina." Sabrina stiffened. It was her stepmother appearing out of nowhere to give her an air kiss. Genevieve looked elegant in a silver dress with one strap over her pale shoulder. She was carrying a small silver clutch bag that probably cost more than Sabrina's dress. "Adam is looking all over for you."

"Oh, really? I just got here, so I really haven't had time to say hello to anyone. Genevieve, this is Zach Prescott."

Genevieve smiled briefly. "Nice to meet you. Would you excuse us, Jack?"

"I'll catch up with you in a few minutes," Sabrina said. "I want to talk to *Zach* for a moment."

Genevieve opened her mouth to say something, but finally shrugged and walked away.

"My stepmother," Sabrina explained.

"Not like the one in Snow White, I hope."

"Oh, no. No 'Mirror, mirror on the wall' and so forth. And no poison apples—at least not yet. Though I must say I do disappoint her from time to time. She wouldn't poison me, but she'd probably like to throttle me sometimes."

"Who's Adam?" Zach asked casually.

"My ex-fiancé."

"Still your ex?" He hoped he didn't sound as gleeful as he felt.

"Still my ex. I think he must realize by now he got off pretty easily by not marrying me. He's really a nice guy, but I would have driven him crazy."

"How do you mean?"

"I'd be complaining about the amount of time he spent at the office, always ditching me to go back to work when I wanted him to go play in the snow, that kind of thing," she said with a smile.

"Not your type at all."

"That's right."

She wondered if Zach was her type. CEO of a company? Not likely.

She looked around at the crowd without really seeing anyone, but not knowing what else to say. She felt Zach's intense gaze on her, but was afraid to look at him. Afraid if she did, he'd know what she was thinking.

She was about to make an excuse to break away, when the blonde she'd seen him with earlier came up and put her hand on his arm.

"Where did you go?" she asked.

"To say hello to an old friend. Pam Gilbert, this is Sabrina White."

Pam shook Sabrina's hand. "Nice to meet you. It's time to get in line for the buffet," she said, wrapping her arm around Zach's. Then she did a double take. "Where did you get the flower?"

"This?" Zach fingered the apple blossom in his buttonhole. "It must have fallen from the tree."

"Hmm," she said with a suspicious glance in the direction of Sabrina's hair.

Zach said goodbye and as they walked away, Sabrina felt a stab of envy through her heart. What was wrong with her? She had no claim on Zach. Sure, they'd had a good time, exchanged a few kisses, but that was all. For all he knew, she was an unreliable woman, the kind who ran away from marriage, not one a guy should get emotionally involved with. For all *she* knew, he was engaged to this Pam person. He never said he wasn't. But he had asked her to bid on him. That had to mean something.

All of a sudden, Sabrina was alone in the crowd. She felt a wave of panic and looked around for the nearest exit. She was so edgy, she was even glad to see Adam.

He kissed her on the cheek. She felt no thrills, no chills, nothing but gratitude for his understanding. They'd had a good talk when she got back, and if he'd been angry, he covered it well. She even wondered if he'd been a little bit relieved that she'd walked out on him, despite what had to be a humiliating moment.

"Ready for dinner?" he asked.

Once again, she was amazed at how well he was taking this whole thing. He could be very charming, which was what had attracted her to him in the first place. That and their similar upbringings. If he wasn't relieved they weren't getting married, was he really just being a good sport? Or was it possible he thought they'd get back together?

"I need to find Meg first," Sabrina said.

"She's in line already."

He hooked his palm around her elbow and they walked toward the tent with the various food stations where black-jacketed waiters carried trays of champagne. Adam snagged two glasses for them.

Maybe after a glass or two of champagne, she'd have the courage to make sure Adam knew it was over between them. As if she hadn't told him already when she got back from the mountains. It didn't hurt to repeat it again, just in case. Because he was acting as though nothing had changed.

But everything had changed. Seeing Zach again, noting the effect he had on her, she knew she could never marry anyone she didn't feel an emotional attachment to, not to mention passion.

She took a sip of champagne. "You're being very nice about this whole thing, Adam. After what I did to you… I want you to know I appreciate it."

"Everyone gets wedding jitters," he said. "We should never have planned such a big wedding. Next time I won't keep you waiting. I've learned my lesson."

Her heart sank. He didn't get it, after all.

"Adam, there's not going to be a next time," she said. "It's over. We're through. I'm not getting married. Not to you, not to anyone."

Sabrina expected him to be hurt by her necessary bluntness. She even expected him to protest. But she didn't expect him to laugh!

"I mean it, Adam." Why didn't he take her seriously?

He squeezed her hand. "I know you do. It's just you're so cute when you get excited. Just relax and don't worry about what happened."

"I'm not worried. I'm *concerned*." She was concerned he didn't believe her, after she'd bared her soul to him, feeling it was the right thing to do to help him understand why she'd done what she did. She knew she shouldn't encourage him in any way. She certainly shouldn't act like his date by eating dinner with him.

"Where'd you get the flower?" he asked, fingering the apple blossom behind her ear.

"That? It must have fallen from the tree," she said.

She glanced around the giant tent at the well-dressed crowd, the scent of expensive perfume overwhelming the apple blossoms. Not a sign of anyone else she knew. Where was Meg? Where were her parents? Where was Zach?

Chapter Seven

Zach glanced around the tent, his gaze instantly drawn to Sabrina standing in the buffet line with a tall man, his head bent in her direction, as if hanging on every word she said. His jaw clenched so tight, he could hardly speak. But he felt compelled to know who the man was. He leaned toward his friend, Chad, and whispered, "Who's the couple over there, the blond guy with the woman in black?"

"That's Sabrina White, the runaway bride. It's a pretty recent scandal. Everyone was talking about it. Guess you were out of town at the time."

Zach was listening to his friend as he sat down between Chad and Pam at a white linen-covered table, but his eyes were on Sabrina. "Is that the guy she left?"

"Yeah, that's him, Adam Barker. I can't believe they're still together."

Zach's stomach lurched and suddenly the shrimp scampi, crab cakes and asparagus spears covered with aoli dressing on his plate looked totally unappetizing. "Are they?" he asked, hoping he didn't sound as interested as he was.

"Looks that way from here, but your guess is as good as mine," Chad said. "I hear her family was livid."

"What was the deal?" Zach asked.

"Probably the usual. Wedding jitters."

"That's all?"

"I don't know. I'll introduce you. You can ask her."

"You know her?"

"Not very well. She's not a partyer. Never shows up at the bars on Union Street. He's a venture capitalist. Some big shot at McNeill Perkins."

Despite his efforts to find out more, the conversation turned to other gossip. Zach forced himself to eat a little and drink some wine. He had no interest in flirting with Pam, so she turned her attention to some other guy while he continued to stare at Sabrina and her ex-fiancé across the room.

He searched his memory, trying to remember what she'd said about her almost-marriage. The most hopeful thing he'd heard tonight was that *she* was the one who'd broken off the engagement— albeit at the last minute. That was one piece of the puzzle that was the runaway bride. Would he ever fill in any more blanks?

Chad tapped him on the shoulder, startling him. "Hey, buddy, time for the auction."

Zach grimaced and stood up. "Already?"

"Afraid no one will bid on you?"

"I couldn't take the humiliation. What about you?"

"I've got someone standing by."

"You mean this thing is rigged?" Zach asked.

"It's all fixed. Who cares, as long as we raise money for charity? Come on, didn't you tell somebody to bid on you?"

He'd asked Sabrina, but what were the chances she'd actually go through with it? Not only was she with her ex, but she and Zach had decided they had no future, so why on earth would she voluntarily spend a weekend with him?

These thoughts went through his mind as he took his place on the stage with Chad and a dozen other bachelors. Using a microphone, the emcee described each of the men, their stats reverberating around the canvas walls of the tent as if they were cattle at a country auction.

"Zach Prescott, MBA, CEO of his own company. Thirty-three years old. Six foot three, one hundred seventy-five pounds of pure muscle. Bench-presses one-forty-five and runs half-marathons."

Zach felt his ears turning red. But the worst was yet to come when the emcee started describing what the winner would get: a weekend at one of various boutique hotels, as well as dinner at the Grand Café. A whole weekend with a stranger? Good grief, when would this nightmare be over?

The bidding for Zach started high and went higher. He took a deep breath and forced a smile. He stared out over the heads of the crowd. He didn't want to see who was bidding on him. Whoever won, he'd have to get out of it somehow. He'd come down with a mysterious disease. He'd join the Foreign Legion. Buy his way out by donating an obscene amount to the hospital charity. Whatever it took.

He heard Pam's voice shouting out a bid higher than all the others. She was a nice woman, but a whole weekend with her? He couldn't do it. He wished a trapdoor would open and he could fall through the stage. Anything would be better than this.

Sabrina stood at the back of the crowd next to Meg. Her heart was beating erratically as the bidding went higher and higher for Zach. She could understand it. He looked so handsome up there and so vulnerable at the same time. Clearly he wanted to be somewhere else. Anywhere else.

"Why don't you bid on your friend?" Meg asked. "I think he'd like it if you did."

"I know, but I can't," Sabrina muttered. "You don't understand," she said, watching his friend Pam raise her hand and up her bid.

"No, I don't," Meg whispered. "I've bid on Granger, and I won him. Now, if you want Adam to realize it's truly over, I say raise your hand."

Meg jostled Sabrina just as the auctioneer looked their way. "Do I hear seven, I see seven-fifty. Going once, going twice, sold to the lady in black at the back."

"Oh, my God," Sabrina murmured. "Now see what you've done."

"See what *you've* done," Meg said with a giggle. "You and I and our dates are in for *some* weekend. I hope you're ready."

Sabrina shivered. Her stomach was full of dancing butterflies. She couldn't look at the stage to see if Zach knew who'd won him. She had to find him and explain that it was all a mistake.

But was it? Wasn't it just what she'd really wanted, a romantic weekend with Zach Prescott?

Like a robot, she pushed her way through the crowd toward the stage. Zach was talking to the auctioneer, probably explaining why he couldn't go through with it.

"Here she is," the auctioneer said as Sabrina approached. "The beautiful lady who won you, Prescott. You lucky dog."

Zach turned and stared. She could tell by his expression that he was surprised to see the winning bidder was her. Then he broke into a broad grin that warmed her inside and out. She felt giddy with relief. He was glad it was her. She grinned back at him.

"Over here, ladies and gentlemen, for the photos," the auctioneer ordered.

Her grin faded as the group of bachelors and their dates were herded onto stage and instructed to put their arms around each other. Not just for the photographer, but for everyone and their brother to see.

As the cameras flashed, Sabrina noticed her father and stepmother looking toward the stage from their table, shocked. She didn't see Adam. She could only hope he'd missed the auction and was somewhere else. Not that he wouldn't hear about it eventually.

What would he think when he found out? What did everyone think? She could just hear the buzz.

She's just dumped her fiancé and here she is bidding on and winning another guy? What's up with that? Where did he come from?

All around her, the couples were laughing and talking and posing for individual couple shots. Meg was beaming at Granger and seemed to have forgotten all about Sabrina. So Meg didn't need her, after all.

When the photographer got to Sabrina and Zach, he shouted out directions. "Arms around each other. Gaze into each other's eyes. Come on, she just paid a fortune to spend a weekend with you."

Sabrina was racked with conflicting emotions. Shock that she'd won Zach. Fear that the whole world would wonder what on earth she was thinking. First running out on her wedding and now, only weeks later, spending a weekend with some other guy.

She wanted to grab the microphone and shout that it wasn't what they thought. That she was only helping out. Helping Meg out. Helping Zach out. Helping the charity out. She was a true philanthropist. All she cared about was others.

Yeah, right. All she could think about right now was herself. Herself and Zach, together for a weekend *without* seven kids. It sounded heavenly and made her whole body hum with a feeling of guilty excitement.

"Hey," the photographer said. "I like the matching flowers. You two plan this?"

They shook their heads "No" in unison.

"Thanks for bidding on me," Zach murmured into her ear. "I know you did it to benefit the hospital, because I know you're here with your fiancé—"

"*Ex* fiancé. We're not engaged anymore."

"Are you sure about that?"

"Positive. But if you're worried about spending a weekend with me…"

"Me, worried? Not a chance. I'm looking forward to it."

"It's just a weekend. No big deal. I think we can handle that," Sabrina said lightly. But could she really handle a weekend with him? Without any kids and guaranteed interruptions? "It should be fun." If she could fool him into thinking it was no big deal, maybe she could fool herself, too.

The photographer moved on. Zach dropped his arm and Sabrina wrote her phone number on a card and gave it to Zach.

"Are you sure you can spare the time for this?" she asked. "I know you missed some work when you were in the mountains. If you want to cancel or postpone, I'll understand." Not only would she understand, she'd be relieved. She'd know then he was just another workaholic and she could stop daydreaming about him. But if she were honest, she'd have to admit she'd be disappointed.

He shook his head. "I think we'd better go through with it. My brother has often pointed out to me that I work too hard. This is my chance to show him I don't. I might even turn off my cell phone."

"That sounds serious," she joked.

His eyes darkened. "Sabrina, before we go off for a weekend, we need to talk."

Sabrina's heart fell. Here it came. The disclaimer. She wished she hadn't used the word *serious*. She didn't want him to think she was serious about *him*. She held her breath, waiting for the other shoe to drop.

But before they could have a conversation of any kind, Sabrina saw Adam striding purposefully toward them.

"Maybe we can talk on the phone. I've got some explaining to do." Then she hurried down the steps to the ballroom floor. She felt Zach's curious gaze follow her, but right now she had more things to worry about than Zach and whatever he thought he had to talk to her about. After all, wasn't he just a ship passing in the night—albeit one that came back for another pass? Whereas Adam had been around for years. Then there were her parents. They'd be really upset.

"What have you done?" Adam asked, staring at her as if she'd just gotten up and done the moonwalk in front of the crowd.

She chuckled self-consciously at the image. "I

just wanted to help out the children's hospital, that's all. Of course, I didn't think, I mean, I didn't intend to win a weekend with anyone."

"You're not going through with it, are you?" he asked.

"Adam, someday, I don't know when, I'm going to start dating again. And so are you. We're simply not right for each other. You know it as well as I do."

He pressed his lips together in a tight line. She knew that look of his. He was shutting out what he didn't want to hear. "I don't believe that," he said.

"You have to believe that. I want someone who's going to be a family man."

"That's me," he said. "Why else would I want to get married?"

"I want a man who's not married to his work."

"You want to marry someone who stays home?" Adam asked incredulously. "How will you live? How will you have the things you want, the house, the cars, the perks? Those don't come out of the sky, you know."

"I know, Adam. But I'm not talking about material things. I'm talking about making memories…together. And as a family. Maybe I'm not being realistic. Maybe I'm just a hopeless dreamer or some kind of romantic. But that's how I feel. I'm sorry I didn't figure it out sooner. It would have saved us both a lot of money, time and anguish. But there you are."

He nodded slowly. "There I am. And there you are, Sabrina, looking pretty darn fabulous in your black dress and flower in your hair, going after some other guy. How is that supposed to make me feel?"

"I'm sorry. But you're wrong. I'm not going after anybody. That's all I can say." What more could she say?

After he finally gave up and walked away, she had to deal with her parents who were waving to her, beckoning her to their table where they'd saved her a place and a piece of the gourmet mile-high apple pie that was a tradition at the ball.

"Another embarrassing scene," her stepmother muttered when Sabrina took a seat between her and her father. "First the wedding and now this."

"I'm really, really sorry about the wedding," Sabrina said, biting her lip. This was at least the one-hundredth time she'd apologized since she returned from the mountains. She knew she'd put them in an embarrassing position. It was not just the money they'd spent, it was the humiliation of having to explain to relatives, friends, and colleagues what had happened and *why* it had happened, when they really didn't understand. "I plan to repay you for it."

"You can repay us by rescheduling the wedding and going through with it this time," Genevieve said.

"That's the one thing I can't do," Sabrina said.

Genevieve pressed her lips together and suddenly frowned at the flower in Sabrina's hair. "Where did that come from?" she asked.

Sabrina smiled. "Out of the trees, I guess. This is the Apple Ball, after all."

"Who is that man you bid on, Sabrina?" her father asked.

"Just one of the bachelors, Dad," she said. "I only bid on him because the money goes to the children's hospital. Isn't that why we're all here?" Of course, she knew it wasn't. It was all about seeing and being seen on the social circuit.

"What are we supposed to tell our friends this time?" Genevieve asked urgently, leaning toward Sabrina, tapping her red manicured nails on the table. "You bidding on a complete stranger."

"Tell them I felt a burst of generosity," she said.

"That the donation includes a weekend with a good-looking guy, well, I guess I'll just have to bite the bullet and do it." She smiled at her stepmother to soften her words, but Genevieve was not amused.

"You speak to her, Harris," Genevieve said with a pointed look at Sabrina's father.

He shook his head. "It looks like it's too late. I just hope no one we know realized it was you."

Sabrina didn't know what else to say, so she concentrated on her dessert. But after she'd finished the pie and a cup of cappuccino and made slightly strained conversation with her parents, she pleaded a headache and took a taxi home. By the time she arrived at her apartment, her head was fine, but she had a pain in her stomach. Too much pie? Something in the apples? Had her stepmother poisoned her like Snow White's had? Ridiculous. She was getting carried away.

By the next morning, she was back to normal.

Until she read the newspaper.

Maybe no one would have known Sabrina had bid on a good-looking hunk and won him, if the pictures hadn't appeared in the social pages. But there she was, with Zach's arm around her, her name and the amount she'd bid on him in the caption for all to read.

Suddenly, his last words echoed in her head. *Sabrina, we have to talk.*

But did she want to hear what he had to say?

Chapter Eight

Sunday came and went with no phone call from Zach. So when her cell phone during recess break at school on Monday, she jumped nervously.

It was Meg.

"I can't believe it. Did you see us in the paper?" her friend enthused.

"I kind of wish they hadn't done that," Sabrina said. "I'm in enough trouble as it is with my parents. First I bail on the wedding, then I make a spectacle of myself Saturday night."

"Tell me about this guy," Meg said. "The one you bid on. The one you're spending the *whole* weekend with in three weeks? And don't tell me he's nobody."

Sabrina noticed it was suddenly quiet in the teachers' lounge, and that anyone who wanted to could hear what she was saying. To escape the curious glances aimed her way, she walked outside to the playground where the children were shouting, running and throwing balls.

"I met him in the mountains."

"Aha. The plot thickens," Meg said. "So that's why he calls you Snow White. No wonder you haven't been yourself since you came back. The guy is a hunk!"

"You think so?"

"I know so. If it weren't for Granger..."

"How did that work out, by the way?"

"Fantastic. I owe it all to you. I never would have had the nerve to go to the ball, let alone bid on him if you hadn't been there. Now you say something nice about me. How you never would have bid on Prince Charming if I hadn't made you do it."

"I'm not sure I've done the right thing," Sabrina said, pacing back and forth at the edge of the playground. "I'm so afraid of making another disastrous mistake. I'm not very good at choosing men, as you may have noticed."

"Everybody deserves a second chance. Especially you," Meg said. "And it looks like you're going to get it."

"Talk to you later, Meg. Recess is over."

When he called her at home on Tuesday night she managed to stay calm. When he said they should talk in person, she readily agreed and gave him her address.

An hour after finally phoning Sabrina, asking to talk in person, Zach dashed up the long flight of stairs to the small apartment on the third floor of an old Victorian in the Cow Hollow neighborhood.

He was in excellent shape, thanks to his health club and the stationary bike in his living room, but he was out of breath by the time he got to Sabrina's front door. Which had nothing to do with the three flights of stairs he'd just climbed. It was the anticipation of seeing her again. She literally took his breath away. And she hadn't even opened the door yet.

When she finally appeared, he saw the Sabrina from the mountains, in a sweatshirt and pants, though these were made for her, clinging to her every curve. He stood for a moment and just stared at her.

"What's wrong?" she asked, taking a step backward.

"Just trying to get a handle on you. First you're Snow White, then Super Nanny, then Cinderella."

"I didn't leave my glass slipper, did I?" she joked. "Come in. Can I get you a cup of coffee? I can make a cappuccino."

"Sounds good." Restless, he walked around the living room while she went to the kitchen. The room was simple but charming. Furnished with big, slip-covered chairs in natural fabrics and a low leather couch. A fireplace with real logs in it. Big bay windows with a view of the bridge. A tall bookcase filled with mysteries and some biographies.

He paused to look at the pictures on the wall. There were none with her ex-fiancé, he was glad to note. But there were pictures of her as a child with her parents.

She came back with two steaming mugs of frothy milk and coffee and handed him one. Her fingers grazed his and he felt a jolt of electricity from her touch. She must have felt something, too, because her eyebrows shot up. Maybe it was static electricity from her carpet. Yeah, right. No use denying, even to himself, that there was something special going on between them. The thought sent a shaft of fear through him. Fear of hurting her. Fear of getting hurt. Fear of getting involved with her. Which made it all the more imperative that he say what he'd come to say.

They had no future together.

"You were a cute kid," he said, prolonging the moment as long as he could.

"Thank you. I keep that picture of me and my parents at Ocean Beach there to remind myself of what a perfect childhood is like. After my mother died, everything changed. When my dad married Genevieve, I was horrified to think he was going to replace my mother. I didn't understand how lonely he must have been, I guess, because he was always at work, but Genevieve didn't seem to mind. Still doesn't. And having her for a step-mother isn't as bad as I thought. She's just different."

"Not the wicked stepmother."

"Oh, no. And I was not the perfect stepdaughter, by any means. From what I remember, I was a little brat and she had every reason to throw me out in the snow, like Snow White, but she didn't."

"What about this picture here? Looks like you're in teacher mode."

"That's my very first class on a field trip to the bird sanctuary, seven years ago. Those kids are in junior high now, and, I have to say, they're doing very well. I don't take credit for it. They were a fantastic bunch. They come back and see me sometimes. It's, well, amazing to think I've been at it this long."

"You show no signs of stopping, Teacher of the Year."

"How do you know about that?"

"You told me to check you out."

"So I did. No, I have no plans to stop teaching. In fact, I intend to keep at it until I'm sixty-five. For women like me without children, it's especially satisfying to help bring up other peoples' kids."

"You're not going to have any of your own?" He'd had her pegged as a future soccer mom, devoted to hearth and home and her husband.

She gave him a little smile. "It doesn't look that way. I obviously have terrible judgment in men—present company excluded, of course. To prevent making another terrible mistake, I intend to stay single. I'm lucky because I have a new group of kids every year who will hopefully keep me feeling young even when I'm a shriveled-up spinster."

He studied her face for a long moment. Was it possible he didn't have to make his speech, after all? Or did he? "I bet you'll be a sexy shriveled-up spinster," he said with an appreciative glance at her undeniably sexy body. Too bad he wouldn't be around to see how she looked at sixty-five.

She grinned. "That's very nice of you to say, I think." She sat in one of the large, slip-covered chairs. "Now what is it we have to talk about? If you want to back out of the weekend, I understand. It was just a crazy impulse. I'm happy just to have made my contribution to charity."

Zach took a seat on the leather sofa across from her, set his cup on an end table and ran a hand through his hair. "No, I didn't come here to tell you I'm backing out. Just the opposite. I'm looking forward to this weekend of ours more than I ever thought I would. There's something between us and I can't just walk away from it.

"Here's my question for you," he said. "How do you feel about me?"

"I don't know what to say. I've been through a lot lately. I'm in no position to take a stand on anything or anyone at this point. You came through for me when I needed it most. I won't forget that."

"So it's just gratitude you feel for me. I guess that answers my question."

She shook her head. "That's not true. I agree, there's something between us. I like you a lot and I'd like to get to know you better. Since I just told you the boring story of my life, I think it's your turn now." She sat back and took a sip of her coffee.

"I wasn't bored," he said. He wondered how much he had to tell, now that he'd found out she wasn't looking for a serious relationship any more than he was. They were both up for a fun weekend, no strings attached. What could be better?

"Well?" she prompted.

He tented his hands. Why not come clean with her? That way, she'd realize where he was coming from, and, more important, where he was going.

"My parents dumped me and my brother off at social services when I was seven and he was five. 'It was just temporary,' they said, 'until they got jobs.' Then they'd be back to get us. Not that life up till then was a picnic. It was one move after another, leaving apartments in the middle of the night to avoid paying the rent. That kind of thing."

"Oh, how awful for you," Sabrina said, her eyes dark with sympathy.

He held up his hand. "Please. No pity. It turned out all right, as you can see. You've met Al, you saw how happy he is. He has a great wife and a houseful of kids. It's obvious he got the life he wanted and you see me here, just as happy with my fate."

"So where did you go? Did your parents come back to get you?"

He shook his head. "I have no idea what happened to them. The state tried to find them, but never could. They disappeared into a dark hole. They were good at that. They'd had lots of practice."

"That must have been…hard. Did you get adopted then?"

"Oh, no. We were not adoptable. We heard that many times over the years. Not just because my parents were still alive, for all anyone knew. But there were other reasons." Even now, the words he'd heard whispered behind their backs rankled. "Unmanageable, disruptive, damaged…I tried to keep Al from hearing, from knowing what they said about us, but I couldn't."

"Which may explain his taking in those seven kids," she said.

"Bingo," Zach said. "Yeah, even now I wonder

if I should have insisted we stay together. If I hadn't, some nice family might have adopted Al. He was younger, he was cuter. He wasn't a problem kid like I was. But I wouldn't let them separate us. So we went from foster home to foster home. Some not bad, some moderately bad. When I turned eighteen, I got custody of Al, put myself through school, got a job and we took care of ourselves. Not exactly the Brady Bunch, but we were a family, him and me."

Zach stretched his legs out in front of him. As unwilling as he'd always been to tell this story to anyone, it wasn't as hard as he'd thought it would be. Sabrina was looking at him so intently, without the pity he'd expected, that he realized he actually wanted her to know his background. He wanted to lay everything out on the table. He felt as if some of the weight had been taken off his shoulders. Weight that had been there for a long, long time.

"So that's my story. I came out of it stronger and tougher and more stubborn than ever. Determined never to let anyone control my life ever again. I'm making enough money to have the life I want. Nobody's ever going to kick me out of an apartment. Although I have no desire to have a life like Al's, I'm proud as hell of him."

Sabrina nodded. Her eyes were suspiciously bright.

"Hey, you're not crying, are you? This is a story with a happy ending."

She nodded. "I know. But you went through so much. I feel like a spoiled princess compared to you. You *should* be proud of Al, and you should be proud of yourself." She reached for a tissue and blew her nose. "Now, what's the moral of the story?"

"The moral, Snow White, is that I'm not the kind of guy any woman would want to get serious about. Because I have no interest in tying myself down to anyone. I don't want any more responsibility than myself. My work is another matter. I've had success in business and I intend to have more. Which means I have more work to do. Fortunately I love my job. Some women have even accused me of being married to my work."

Sabrina gave him a wry smile.

"There," he said, draining his mug and getting to his feet. "I've told you more than you wanted to know about Zach Prescott."

"Not quite. You haven't said anything about the women in your life."

"Because there aren't any. None that matter."

"What about love?" she asked.

"Love?" He gave a hollow laugh. "I'm afraid I have to pass on that one. I don't believe in love. No need to ask you the same question, huh? After all, you were going to get married. I assume it had something to do with love."

"I thought I was in love. That's why I was going to marry Adam. But now I think it was more a matter of convenience and comfort. The same kind of family, the same schools, the same social standing. All those things that don't matter in the long run if you don't share the same values. If you don't want the same things. I'm just sorry for everyone involved that I didn't figure it out sooner."

"If you had, I wouldn't have met you that snowy day you knocked on my door."

"That's right." She stood and faced him. "So, we both know where we stand. We'll have a pleasant weekend together and that's it. No ties, no strings, no future."

He tilted his head and gave her a long, intense look. Then he held out his hand. "Ships that pass in the night. Let's shake on it."

Sabrina held out her hand, but they didn't shake on it. Instead, he pulled her into his arms and kissed her. Just a brief feathered kiss on the lips. Then he bent his head and kissed her hard and deep. She ought to stop him. Especially now that she knew how he felt about love and marriage. But stopping him was the last thing on her mind. This was what she wanted. His arms around her, his hot, hungry mouth on hers.

It felt so good, so right. She kissed him back. Giving him the impression she wanted more. She did. She did. How was she going to keep her emotional distance from this man if they went at it as if there were no tomorrow? Because there was a tomorrow and another after that. Gasping for breath, fighting for some kind of control, she pulled away and stared into his dark eyes, waiting, wondering, wanting him to kiss her again, her whole body aching for more.

But she couldn't have more. She'd already gone farther than she should with a man like him. So instead of standing there, waiting for something that wasn't going to happen, she made herself walk to the door and open it for him. She watched him walk down the stairs, before racing to the window to see him get into his car. He looked up and waved to her.

Her heart knocked against her ribs. The hand

that she held in the air to wave at him was shaking. Even after their long talk, unspoken questions hung in the air. What happened if one of them changed his mind? What if one of them fell in love? What then?

She knew the answer to that one. *Don't* fall in love.

She sank onto her sofa and buried her face in her hands. Too late. Too late. She had a sinking but overwhelming feeling that she'd already fallen in love with a man who didn't believe in love. Why had he told her the story of his life? Why had he opened up like that? He'd pushed her over the edge from attraction, to like to love.

She'd just made the second biggest mistake of her life.

Chapter Nine

Two and a half weeks later, Sabrina and Zach stepped into the lobby of the Emperor Norton Inn on a quiet one-way street just off Union Square in downtown San Francisco. It was Friday night at five o'clock and they were just in time for a glass of California wine in the lobby, which was accented with rich reds and comfy couches. Sabrina had hoped the prize included a big, impersonal hotel, since she didn't need to be surrounded by charm and romance for a weekend with a man who didn't believe in love. But she was out of luck. This place was small, romantic and charming. Just the kind of hotel you'd want to go to with the love of your life. If such a person existed.

Sabrina was just as glad to stop in the lobby for a glass of wine and postpone seeing their room. She got the shakes just thinking about the possibility of a king-size bed and nothing else. Surely the hotel wouldn't assume… No. Still, she couldn't put the image out of her mind. She'd have to insist on taking the couch.

If there was a couch.

After the encounter in her apartment, she'd been dreading this weekend. So far, she was proud of herself for her ability to make lighthearted conversation on the drive to the hotel. Especially after the day she'd had at school.

Zach, whatever his day had been like, was good at pretending nothing at all had happened between them. Or maybe he wasn't pretending. Maybe in his view, nothing earthshaking had happened.

"Nice place," he said, looking around the lobby at the string trio in the corner playing classical music and the gas lamps on the walls. "Ever been here before?"

She shook her head. "No. It's lovely."

He took a swallow of wine. "Shall we see what the room is like?"

Sabrina almost choked on the excellent pinot noir in her glass. "So soon?" she asked.

He grinned. "We have a lot on our schedule. Dinner, dancing. At least that's what's planned, right?"

Sabrina's knees went weak. "Uh, right, I guess so." What did he expect from her? If he thought this weekend included a roll in the hay, she was going to have to set up a list of Don'ts. She'd already prepared them in her mind.

No kissing.

No hugging.

No unnecessary touching.

And definitely no sex.

She reached into her tote bag and handed him the schedule she'd written up.

"Looks like we're supposed to play tourist," he said. "Ride the cable car, stroll around the Wharf, have five-course dinner at the Grand Café. And that's just tonight."

"That's right." No use getting herself tied up in knots. He was a sensitive guy. She knew him well enough to know he'd never push her into doing anything she didn't want to. But, God help her, she *wanted* to do all those things on her Don't list!

Their accommodations turned out to be the two-room Royal Penthouse Suite. Sabrina stood in the doorway, awestruck. She wasn't unfamiliar with luxury hotels, but this was beyond all her expectations. The hotel had been more than generous. Zach, too, was speechless. After the aged but venerable bellman had deposited their luggage and lighted a fire in the hearth, described the original 1912 stained glass skylight and opened the patterned draperies to show off the panoramic views of the city, he then proceeded to tell them a few true-life stories about the historic suite.

"Some of the famous couples who honeymooned here are movie stars and governors, even a president and his mistress. Discretion forbids me from mentioning any names, of course."

"Of course," Sabrina murmured, but she wondered who it could have been.

"I *can* mention His Highness Prince Frederic of Romania, one of the signers of the UN Charter, who stayed here in 1945 with his retinue. But enough of history. I'm sure you'll make your own history here with us at the inn. Remember, the walls can't talk." With that he winked and discreetly bowed out of the room, just as he might have done after carrying up the president's mistress's luggage.

"I see there have been a few upgrades since the prince was here," Zach said, opening a cabinet to find a large flat-screen TV inside.

"I think I've gotten much more than my money's worth," Sabrina said.

"I'll have to make sure you do," Zach said.

They stood shoulder to shoulder at the window, gazing out at the twinkling lights of the city. There was something in his tone that made her glance at him. There was a gleam in his eyes that started her heart pounding. Was now the time to state the list of Don'ts? Before she'd forgotten what they were?

"Zach, I've been thinking…"

He turned and put his hand over her mouth. "Now is not the time to think, Snow White. We've got better things to do. Remember, the walls can't talk."

"Yes, but…" She stopped. The look in his eyes told her what he had in mind. She had to make it clear what this weekend was about and what *wasn't* going to happen. She removed his hand from her lips and took a deep breath. But just as she opened her mouth to make her speech, he showed that he was way ahead of her.

"Sabrina," he said, his eyebrows drawn together. "In case you're worried, I'm planning on sleeping on this pullout sofa."

"Oh, no. You take the bed. The last time—"

"The last time you were recovering from hypothermia and God knows what else. This time, you're the princess. You get the canopy bed with the satin sheets and the goose down pillows."

"Now how do you know about those?" she asked.

"I read the brochure in the lobby," he said. "Want to check it out?"

She glanced at the bed in the other room, then quickly looked away. The image of sleeping there with Zach was too much for her overloaded psyche. She felt a little feverish. Time to get out of this room with all of its temptations. Temptation one: to take a leisurely soak in the hot tub. Temptation two: a romp between those satin sheets. It didn't help to imagine the romantic trysts that had come before.

Sabrina entered the bedroom and sat on the edge of the canopied bed to change her shoes.

She had to show herself she could do it and not think about getting into that bed with him. It was *not* going to happen.

She reread the itinerary because she was having a hard time remembering what she'd written up to avoid any when her focus had been on what they were *not* supposed to do.

"I confess, as a native San Franciscan, I've only taken the cable car once when I had some out-of-towners to show around. As for Fisherman's Wharf, could anything be more touristy?"

"I've always avoided it. As well as the cable cars," he confessed.

"What about the Grand Café? That's where we're supposed to have dinner at eight."

"Never been there, either. Looks like this will be a weekend filled with new experiences," he said, entering the bedroom. He took her hand in his, stroking her palm with his thumb. She looked up at him. Their eyes met and held. She knew what he was doing. Seducing her. And he probably thought he could, if he could hear the way her heart was beating a staccato rhythm. What if he kissed her again? Oh, Lord, she was in such big trouble. It was only Friday night. How was she going to get through the next two days?

She summoned all her willpower and jumped off the bed. Then she went to her suitcase and pulled out a thick sweater to put over her shirt and jeans, tossed a scarf on, and suggested they head out. A little brisk San Francisco air ought to clear away these unwanted romantic ideas of hers.

The speed of the little cable cars that went "halfway to the stars" was only nine and a half miles an hour, but when they crested the hill and looked straight down the almost perpendicular street into the Bay, it felt as if they were back on the toboggan in the mountains heading down a slippery slope.

They stood on the outside platform, hands wrapped around the metal safety bar. Zach had one arm around her, and at the sharp turns she clung to him, burying her face in his leather jacket, feeling safe and scared at the same time. He smelled so good, all leather and sandalwood. He looked so sexy with his hair blowing in the wind. The views of the city and the Bay and the bridge strung with lights were spectacular. But Sabrina had a hard time forcing herself to look anywhere but at Zach.

"So this is what it's like to be a tourist in San Francisco," he murmured in her ear. "If I'd known,

I might have tried it before. But I didn't know you then. How did I get so lucky?"

Flirting. That was all it was, Sabrina thought. Enjoy it, because it won't last any longer than this weekend. He didn't want anything permanent. And she no longer trusted her judgment where men were concerned.

When they got off the cable car, they wandered along Fisherman's Wharf with hordes of other tourists who stopped to buy take-out shrimp cocktails and stared at the street mimes who posed like statues, then suddenly reached out to startle passersby. They looked at the sidewalk vendors' jewelry.

It was noisy, fun and not romantic. Not at all. Well, except for Zach holding her hand so tightly.

They paused to look at the fishing boats bobbing in the marina. A dinner cruise yacht was pulling in. "I bet you've never been on that, either," he said.

"Of course not. I'm a native," she said with a grin. She knew she should pull her hand away right now and stuff it in her pocket, but she didn't. They leaned over the railing to watch the passengers board. "I'm sure the food would be mediocre at best."

"Probably too cold out there for you, too."

"Too cold for Snow White?" she said. "Not likely. You know, we may never get another chance for a moonlight cruise."

"Why, Ms. White, are you suggesting… You'd give up dinner at the Grand Café?"

"It might be fun to just jump aboard. Going back to the hotel and putting on fancy clothes suddenly doesn't appeal to me. But, look, it's your weekend. If you want to—"

"It's *our* weekend," he said, squeezing her hand.

"Yes, but you're the one who had to put himself on the auction block. That can't have been easy."

"It was a lesson in humility when I thought no one was going to bid on me."

"Are you kidding? The women were all over you."

"I'm glad you won," he said, suddenly serious.

"Me, too," she said. "Anyway, we don't have to stick to the schedule. We can do whatever we want."

"That depends on what we want," he said. "And I think we both want the same thing."

Oh, no, there it was again. The truth. Because she wanted him and he wanted her.

With a blast of the baritone horn, they sailed

into San Francisco Bay. It was cool and breezy out on the water. Sabrina buttoned her bulky hand-knit sweater, wrapped her scarf around her neck and stood at the polished wood railing with Zach.

They watched as the city lights faded in the distance as the boat headed toward the Golden Gate Bridge. The moon shone on the water and the sounds of the orchestra wafted out to the deck. Most everyone else had gone inside, but Sabrina didn't want to break the spell of the moon, Zach's arm around her, the cool air on her face and the feeling of isolation as they moved farther from shore.

"I feel like we're drifting away from real life," she said, watching the waves slap against the side of the boat.

"Is that good?" he asked.

"Today it is. Maybe there is something to be said for living in a fairy tale."

"You ought to know," he said.

"There are some days when I wonder… Today was one of them."

Zach heard a slight tremor in Sabrina's voice. "Let's go in and get something to eat. Then you can tell me about it."

"It's nothing," she murmured as he held the

glass door open for her to the dining room, where the buffet supper was being served. It wasn't five-star dining, but they heaped their plates with a selection of fish, meat and salads and found a small table by a window. After a waiter had filled their wineglasses, Zach watched out of the corner of his eye to make sure Sabrina was okay.

"Now tell me what happened," he said.

She looked up, obviously trying to decide what to say, if anything. He was beginning to understand her. She was a private person, but she was also open and trusting. He wanted her trust. It surprised him how much he wanted it. And he wanted her to know he didn't take it for granted, but that he deserved it.

She set her fork down. "Since you asked... It was parent-teacher conferences this week and today my favorite kid's parents came in."

Her eyes filled with sudden tears. Alarmed, he reached for his handkerchief.

She took it and wiped her eyes. "He's not the best student. In fact, he's a real handful. Brings in things for show-and-tell that I suspect aren't really his. Shows off on the playground. Tells stories that can't possibly be true. On the other hand, he's as bright as a button. Catches things no one else does. He surprises me. Delights me."

"Sounds a little like me," Zach muttered. "Although I doubt I delighted any of my teachers. But lying? Oh, yeah, I get that. Sometimes the truth is not what people want to hear."

"I thought about that. I thought about what you told me about your childhood. Unlike you, this kid has two parents. But they're getting a divorce. That's what they told me today. In fact, we didn't talk about Charlie hardly at all. That's how self-absorbed they are. It was all about them. Why is it the wrong people have kids?" she asked.

"Good question," he said. "One I've asked myself many times. But he sounds like he's coping."

"As best he can. At least now I understand why he acts out the way he does. Now I can help him more."

"How?"

"I don't know. I'm just starting to think."

"Maybe I could do something with him. I've got experience with kids. Al will give me a good reference."

"You'd do that?" Her eyes widened. Her smile was worth a lot.

But, wait. What was he doing? Volunteering to help some kid he didn't even know? "If you think it would do any good. And if the parents agree."

She nodded. "I'll see what they say. They might reject any outside help, but they might be grateful."

She picked up her fork and took a bite of salad. "I hope you don't mind me unloading my prob lems on you. I feel better just talking about it. And I appreciate your offer. Now it's your turn. How was your day?"

He sipped his wine. His natural inclination was to say, "Nothing," or "The usual." After all, how many people really wanted to hear about his problems? But after she'd been so frank and up front with him, he might as well give it a try.

"I lost a big account today."

"What? You look so…so okay. If you're hurting, you do a good job of concealing it."

"Years of practice," he said. "I wouldn't have said anything if you hadn't asked. I don't usually spill my guts, but… Well, this was something I expected, but still, it means laying off a few people. I hate that. I get this tight feeling in my chest that brings back all my old insecurities."

"I can't believe you still have any."

"I don't. Not really. But telling someone he's out of work reminds me of my dad coming home without any money. Of my mother crying. Not that it's going to happen to these guys. They're bright. They're skilled. They'll get other jobs. At least, I hope they will. I told them today."

She reached for his hand across the table. "That couldn't have been easy."

The waiter came to remove their plates and pour their coffee. Sabrina pulled her hand away and stirred cream into her coffee. Zach sat back in his seat and smiled at her. "Thanks for listening. Somehow I feel better."

"I didn't do anything," she said with a shrug.

"Yes, you did. You listened. You understood." So this was what it was like to share your days with someone. Not just anyone, but someone special. He'd never known. Never wanted to know what it was like. It might get habit-forming. "Enough being serious. Want to dance?"

She nodded.

He wasn't much of a dancer. And it wasn't easy dancing on a moving boat, but if the objective was to have an excuse to hold Sabrina in his arms—and it was—it worked. They glided, they stumbled, they laughed, and he spun her around. Then the music turned slow and dreamy. He pressed her tight against him, and felt her warm cheek against his shirt and her heart beating in time with his. As if they belonged together.

They didn't. He didn't belong to anyone. He didn't belong *with* anyone. Yes, he liked her. Of course he wanted her. Who wouldn't? She was sweet, caring, gorgeous, smart and sexy. He'd volunteered to help a kid in her class, but that didn't mean *they* had any future together. After this weekend, he'd pull away. He had to. Because this feeling of closeness, this wanting someone, this needing someone, was *no* good.

Before he was ready, before they'd had a chance to stroll the deck again, the cruise was over. They staggered off the boat into the darkness. Had they really drunk so much wine? Or was it making the transition from sea to land?

Or was it the transition from friends to something else that had put him off balance?

All he could think about was that big bed with the satin sheets and the down pillows and Sabrina with her dark hair spread out on the pillow. He knew what she looked like nearly naked. That image was seared into his brain forever.

They made the trip back to the hotel by cable car. As they walked down the dark one-way street, they were surprised to see a limousine with diplomatic plates parked in the circular brick driveway. A small crowd had gathered on the sidewalk. They heard bits and pieces of conversation.

"Who is it?"

"Somebody important."

"Royalty, I heard."

"But who?"

"What's going on?" Zach asked the doorman.

The tall, imposing uniformed doorman beckoned them inside, then escorted them to the manager who was standing behind the front desk.

"Oh, Ms. White," he said, his forehead beaded with perspiration. "I have bad news for you. There's been a terrible mix up. Prince Frederic of Romania is in the city for medical treatment. We had no idea he was coming. Of course we had to give him his usual accommodations. Your room. I hope you understand."

Sabrina's face paled. "Of course," she said. She looked at Zach. He shrugged. What else could she say? What else could they do?

"Don't worry," the manager said. "We've moved your luggage. You and Mr. White are in the King George Room. Very nice. Not a two-room suite, but it has a terrace and king-size feather bed. You'll like it, I know."

Sabrina licked her dry lips. Mr. *White*. A one-room suite? A mix up. As in one bed? No fold-out couch? What about a rollaway bed? How had this happened? Now what were they going to do?

Sabrina braced her hand against the polished walnut front desk, took the key to the King George room in her hand and drew a deep, shaky breath. One way or another, this was going to be a night to remember.

Chapter Ten

The room was charming, with its cozy, provincial blue-and-tan decor, eighteenth-century furnishings and a huge chandelier right out of *Phantom of the Opera*. But it was one room, with one large, four-poster bed, turned down to reveal luxurious cream-colored sheets and a chocolate truffle on each pillow.

What could she say, but enthuse over the arrangements.

"Aren't the fresh flowers beautiful? What a lovely rug!" she exclaimed while her brain was whirling. How, where, when would they go to bed?

"Tired?" he asked.

"No. Not really." Anything to postpone the inevitable.

"Don't worry about the bed. I'll be fine in this chair."

It was a big chair, but not that big. "I can't let you do that."

"We'll trade. You take the bed tonight, I'll take it tomorrow night."

"Well, okay."

"Why don't I go down to the bar and give you a break." He opened the bathroom door and looked inside. "Maybe you'd like a bath in the claw-foot tub?"

Before she could say yes or no, he was out the door. Probably *he* was the one who needed a break. From the minute she'd fallen into his life that night in the mountains, she'd consistently put him in a difficult position. He was a good sport about it, but maybe it was times such as these he really needed to be somewhere else.

She took her small cosmetic bag, along with her cell phone, into the bathroom. She hadn't intended to turn her phone on this weekend, knowing what a turn*off* it was to have it ring in the middle of a romantic moment. But as she was trying her best to *avoid* romantic moments, maybe it wouldn't hurt. Besides, she was dying to know what had happened to Meg and Granger. Where had they ended up? How was their weekend progressing?

She ran a bath using the lavender-perfumed bath salts, submerged her body, then dialed Meg's number.

"Sabrina, where are you?"

"At the Emperor Norton Inn on Sutter. Where are you?"

"Down the street at the Golden Horn."

"What's it like?"

"Divine. We're having the best time." She giggled.

"Am I interrupting something?" Sabrina asked, feeling a pang of jealousy. If only Zach were part of her future the way Granger was most likely going to be part of Meg's.

"No. Tell me how it's going."

"Fine." She sank lower into the water. "Only… oh, Meg, I am *really* in over my head."

"But that's good. That's where you want to be. This is the weekend you paid for. Go for it. Get your money's worth."

"Oh, I am. Even if we went home right now,

I'd have to say it was worth every penny. He's a great guy, Meg. Better than I thought."

"Wow. You mean, no cell phone? No urgent messages from his office? No cancellations? No last-minute changes in the plans? No excuses for being late? With those looks? Snap him up. This guy is too good to be true."

Sabrina blinked back tears. "Not quite. He doesn't want to get married and he doesn't want kids."

"Oh, Sabrina, you'll change his mind."

"I don't think so. Oh, Meg, I'm in so much trouble."

"Sabrina, I've got to go. How about the four of us meet for breakfast tomorrow at Sears on Powell for Swedish pancakes, say, about ten o'clock?"

"It's a date. But promise you won't say anything."

"You know me." Another giggle and she hung up.

Sabrina wished she felt like giggling. Instead, she only felt her stomach churn with anxiety. When she heard a knock at the door, she got up so fast, she splashed water all over the floor. She grabbed a thick terry cloth robe, wound a towel around her hair and went to answer it. She thought

Zach must have forgotten his key. But it was room service instead.

"Compliments of the management," the white-jacketed waiter said, wheeling a cart into the room. "With deepest apologies from the hotel for the mix-up. The manager hopes you will enjoy a glass of bubbly."

He uncorked the champagne, then turned and left before Sabrina could offer him a tip. On his heels, Zach appeared, looking relaxed and rakish at the same time. Why couldn't there be something wrong with him…besides his aversion to commitment? Why couldn't he have a raucous voice or an irritating laugh? No, he had to be smart, engaging and sexy as sin.

"What's this?" he asked, turning the bottle in its silver bucket.

"I think they're trying to make up for the loss of the penthouse suite."

He lifted the lid on a silver tray to reveal pâté, smoked trout, a selection of cheeses and a loaf of warm sourdough bread.

"Mmm," he said, lifting his head and sniffing the air. "You smell like flowers."

"Thanks," she said. "Lavender bath salts. They think of everything."

The way he was looking at her made her wonder if *he* thought of everything, too. She clutched her robe tightly about her. It wouldn't take much, just a tug on the sash, and she'd be naked. But he might as well have undressed her. His long, slow, lingering look made her feel as if he could see right through the terry cloth.

"Hey, nice hat," he teased.

She was so rattled, she'd forgotten about the towel wrapped around her head. She peeled it off and tossed it on the bed, conscious that her hair must be a damp, tangled mess.

He dragged the big overstuffed chair to the small walnut table and grabbed the towel from the champagne bottle to put over his arm like a sommelier. "After you, Madam. A little champagne. A taste of pâté?"

He lowered his voice seductively and suddenly her knees were so weak she had to sit down. He poured the champagne into two flutes and pulled up a straight-backed chair for himself from the small elegant writing desk.

"Just in time. You look weak from hunger," he said.

"It hasn't been *that* long since we ate."

"It must be the hot water."

"How was the bath?"

"Hot."

He grinned and tapped his glass against hers. "To hot water," he said. "May we get into just enough to make life interesting."

She felt a flutter in the pit of her stomach. How could he look at her like that, flirt with her, share his life's secrets with her and know they had no future together? Easy. Lots of practice. Lots of determination.

"To the prince," she countered. There, that was safe.

"I wonder how he's doing," Zach said, leaning back in his chair. "Think he gets a midnight snack delivered to his suite, too?"

"I hope so."

"I hope he's got someone to share it with."

"Don't royals travel with an entourage?"

"Not the same as a beautiful woman."

"Maybe he's got one of those, too," she suggested.

"At one hundred?" he joked. "More power to him. When I'm one hundred—"

"Where do you see yourself?"

She wanted to tell him he could be alone and lonely if he didn't change his mind about his future. But before she could blurt out something she'd be sorry for, the phone rang.

Sabrina shot him an inquisitive look. She felt her blood pressure rise. Just a gut response from all those times when it would be someone from his office for Adam.

"It can't be for me," he said. "No one knows I'm here."

Sabrina walked over and picked up the phone.

"Miss White? This is Prince Frederic."

Sabrina returned to the chair and sat down with a thud. She raised her eyebrows and pointed a finger in the direction of the penthouse suite. Zach got up and stood next to her, his ear to the receiver, one arm looped around her shoulders.

"I must apologize to you and your husband for dislodging you from the suite." His voice was weak and heavily accented.

"Oh, he's not my…that's…perfectly…quite all right," Sabrina stammered. "We're very comfortable where we are."

"I wish to invite you to come up for coffee tomorrow so that I may apologize in person."

"That's not necessary," she said. Zach nodded vigorously.

"I will expect you at ten o'clock, if that is convenient," he said.

"Very convenient," she said. "Thank you."

When she hung up, she stared at Zach. "I've never met a prince in person before."

"Straight out of a fairy tale," he said with a grin. "But don't think he's that prince who wakes you up with a kiss. Remember, he's got to be close to one hundred. Too old to wake up sleeping damsels. If you need to be waked up…" He framed her face with his hands and looked deep into her eyes. "You've got me."

Sabrina tried not to imagine what it would be like to be awakened by Zach with a kiss, next to her in a four-poster bed, but she couldn't help glance toward that luxurious and inviting bed. If only this fairy tale had a happy ending. But it didn't. They had the weekend. That was it. After this, she had to tell Zach she couldn't see him again. What was the point of torturing herself further? He'd made it abundantly clear how he felt about love and marriage. And if she'd learned anything from running out on one wedding already, it was to hold out for the right person the next time.

Zach tilted her head back with his thumbs on

her temples, and she knew what would happen next. One of those soul-searching kisses he was so good at and she was so powerless to resist. Why resist them? Why not give in? It was just one weekend. She burned. She ached. She felt an over-whelming need to have his arms around her, his mouth on hers.

"Oh, Zach," she murmured, before his mouth came down on hers, followed by slow, deep, heart-stopping kisses that melted what little resistance she had. She linked her arms around his neck and pressed her terry cloth-robed body against his.

Adrenaline rushed through her veins. She kissed him fervently, frantically. She forgot every-thing except the man she was kissing, the man she wanted but couldn't have.

She felt more a part of him than anyone she'd ever known. She staggered backward. He followed until they hit the edge of the bed and fell onto it.

The sash to her robe loosened and she was naked.

Zach braced himself with one arm on the mattress. His breathing was ragged. He couldn't do this. Couldn't make love to her, but, oh, how he wanted to. He'd never wanted anything more than he wanted Sabrina. But she was not just any woman. If he made love to her, she'd think he was in love with her. She deserved better.

He kissed the hollow of her throat and pulled her robe around her. Consideration, not passion, was what was needed here. He'd gotten carried away. So had she. She looked at him, her eyes full of questions.

He stared down at her. "Sabrina…" he began. "I want to make love to you, but…"

She sat up abruptly and looked at him with narrowed eyes. "Don't explain," she muttered. "I understand. You're not in the market for a one-night stand, definitely not a two-night stand, and neither am I. We're here to have a good time. That's all. I think we both need a good night's sleep."

He glanced at the chair. No good night's sleep for him. But it wouldn't be the fault of the chair. The thought of her sleeping so close and yet so far was going to play havoc with his libido. He'd seen just enough of her warm, soft body to send his desire into overdrive. His heart was banging against his ribs even now. Those kisses he could still feel on his lips didn't help, either.

Summoning all the strength he had, he got off the bed, retrieved his shaving kit and headed for the bathroom. If she knew what was good for her—for both of them—she'd get into a flannel granny gown and disappear under that quilt before he came out of the bathroom.

When he exited the bathroom after a shower and shave, he had no idea what she was wearing, because, thank God, she'd all but disappeared under the quilt. All he could see was a cloud of hair on the pillow. He knew how soft and silky it would feel if he ran his fingers through it, but he also knew he wasn't going to touch her.

He noticed she'd put a pillow and a blanket on the chair for him. As if they were going to help him sleep. Wearing a T-shirt and boxers, he settled into his chair. With his feet propped on an ottoman, it wasn't that bad.

He stared at Sabrina from across the room. The memory of her first night in the mountains came rushing back. How he'd sat in the living room, watching her on the couch, worried whether she'd be okay. Wondering who in the hell she was and how she'd gotten there.

Now he knew. What he didn't know was how she'd gotten closer to him than anyone else. Was there a void in his life that she filled? No way. He'd made sure there were no voids in his life. It was just circumstances. She'd found him when she needed a place to stay. He'd found her at his door when he needed a hand with the kids. Then there was the fact that they lived in the same city. They'd been bound to run into each other at one time or another. Call it fate. Call it destiny. Or simply call it circumstance. He might even call it luck. Because no matter what happened this weekend, she was a ray of sunshine in a gray foggy city.

He couldn't explain the fireworks that exploded when they were together. He couldn't explain why he'd told her his life story when he'd never told anybody else. And he certainly couldn't explain why he couldn't stand the idea of her marrying any other guy but him.

He turned out the light. He shifted to one side. He closed his eyes, then opened them again. The moon shone through the window, making shadows in the room, turning an ordinary hotel room into a romantic love nest. And sending a shaft of light into his eyes. Served him right. What was he doing sharing a room with a woman he was hot for? He deserved to suffer. He bounded out of his chair and snapped the curtain closed.

"Zach?" Her voice was muffled by the quilt over her head.

"Uh-huh."

"You can't sleep on that chair."

"Sure I can, now that I've shut out the damned moonlight."

She sat up in bed and he could just make out that she was wearing a low-cut nightgown with spaghetti straps. He jerked his head away and stared at the wall. But he couldn't stop his blood pressure from ratcheting up a few notches.

"I was thinking that since neither of us is going to get married—"

"Wait a minute. *I'm* not getting married, but you are." The thought made him feel sick, but he continued, "You're beautiful, kind, and you love kids. Of course, I don't know if you can cook or clean, but…"

He couldn't make out her face, but he could imagine her smile. "Just so you know, I'm no good at either. So there you are. What I was going to say was that since neither of us is getting married, maybe we can be friends."

"I don't think so," he said. Feeling as low as if

he'd just lost his best friend, he sank down in his chair again and accidentally tossed the blanket onto the floor instead of over his feet. Why prolong the agony? After this weekend, he was not going to see her again. Might as well be clear about it. He couldn't be friends with someone he wanted to make love to.

There was a long silence. He didn't say anything to break it. There was nothing to say.

"Well, if that's the way you feel," she said at last. There was hurt and embarrassment in her voice that made his gut churn. "I guess it's best to be brutally frank about these things."

"I didn't mean to be brutal."

She slid down under the covers. "It doesn't matter. You're right, of course."

She didn't say another word.

And neither did he.

Chapter Eleven

At six o'clock, Zach jumped out of his chair when he heard the door to their room close. Disoriented, he looked around. She was gone. He opened the door. The hall was empty.

Damn, he shouldn't have been so brutally frank. He'd hurt her feelings and now she'd run out. One good sign was that her suitcase was still in the room.

After a quick shower, he changed into khakis and a wool sweater, then took the stairs two at a time to the lobby. Sabrina was just coming through the glass entrance doors, holding a paper bag and two paper cups. She smiled at him and his heart turned over. The sun wasn't shining on fog city that morning, but in her sweater and slacks she looked like sunshine and fresh air and everything that was good in the world. How she could manage that before she'd even had coffee was beyond him.

"Breakfast," she announced.

"I thought we were having breakfast with the prince."

"I couldn't wait," she said, sending him a killer smile that set his pulse hammering. "I thought we could go to Union Square and have our coffee and feed doughnut crumbs to the pigeons," she said brightly. "The city looks so different before anybody's awake."

He nodded and held the door open for her.

Union Square, in the heart of downtown San Francisco, was named in honor of the soldiers who fought for the union in the Civil War. Zach and Sabrina weren't the only ones there that early on a foggy Saturday morning. There was a collection of tourists dressed for summer in sandals and shorts in a city that doesn't have summer. There were locals bundled up warmly, reading their newspapers. And there were merchants setting up booths to sell everything from scarves to jewelry to fresh flowers.

It was relatively quiet until the cable cars started clattering past them on Powell Street.

Zach motioned to a bench. They sat down and he knew he had some explaining to do. "About last night…"

Sabrina tensed.

She took a sip of hot coffee, possibly not the right way to calm her nerves, but she had to do something. "You didn't sleep well, I'm sure. Well, tonight you get the bed."

"That's not what I was going to say. I just want to be clear about one thing. The reason I can't be friends with you—"

"Please, don't explain. You'll only make it worse. The way I figure it, I'm getting the karma I deserve. I walked out on somebody who didn't deserve to be stood up at the altar, now you tell me there's nothing for us. I understand. You must think I'm totally unreliable, and a lot of people would agree with you. It's no more or less than I deserve. I can accept that. I ought to be able to. I'm a big girl, after all."

He put a hand on her shoulder. She felt the warmth clear through her sweater and shirt. To show she understood he didn't mean anything by it, she gave him a cool smile.

"That's not it," Zach said. "If I were anybody but me, I'd get down on my knees and beg you to marry me."

"Why?"

"Why? Because you're you. You're everything a man could want."

"But you don't want me."

He groaned. "If you only knew how much I want you. That's why we can't be friends. You're temptation. You're testing my resistance. You're going to be the death of me."

Sabrina leaned back on the bench and sighed. Why didn't she just walk away from him? Why didn't she just call off the weekend right now? What was the point of subjecting both of them to this torture? She slid a sideways glance in his direction. His eyebrows slanted downward. He looked as if he'd just eaten the poison apple meant for Snow White. Yes, he really did look miserable.

Her heart lurched. She wanted to throw her arms around him and tell him she understood. At the same time, she wanted to take him by the shoulders and shake some sense into him. And tell him to leave the past behind. To move on. To take a chance on life. On her.

She did none of those things. She wrenched her gaze away from him and stared at her shoes.

She didn't get it. Not really. She understood about his childhood. She understood how he'd suffered. But his brother had come out of it and he was fine. She could see that Zach was avoiding marriage and commitment because he was afraid of getting hurt again. Of being abandoned again. Of relying on someone who wasn't going to be there for him. That wasn't news. He'd probably admit that in a nanosecond.

But if he'd just give her a chance, she'd be there for him forever. Oh, sure. Like he'd believe that. After what she'd done to Adam. But this was different. She'd never felt this way about Adam. She loved Zach. The terrible part was that she thought he loved her, too. He just didn't know it. And even if he did, he would never admit it. Not to himself and definitely not to her.

"I'm sorry," she said and reached for his hand. "Sorry we can't be friends. But I understand. After this weekend, I go this way." She scraped a line on the bench with the coffee stirrer. "And you go your way." She drew a parallel line next to it.

"I'll still try to help that kid in your class, though."

"If it works out, that would be great." She stood and brushed the crumbs off her lap. The pigeons swooped down and gobbled them up. "Maybe we could take a walk before we meet the prince," she suggested.

They strolled up Post Street, looking in the window of the upscale Gump's Department Store with its place settings of Limoges china, sterling silver tableware and Chinese vases filled with exotic flowers. Strangely enough, they both admired a colorful set of dishes from the south of France with flowers and vines decorating the rims of the plates.

"Cheerful," Sabrina said, pressing her nose against the glass.

"If I ever ate at home, I'd get something like that," he said.

"Where do you eat?"

"At the office, or at the corner coffee shop on my way home."

Sabrina cringed. Again, no home life. He had no sense of what he was missing. Or did he?

"That's what my stepmother has," Sabrina said, pointing to a classic pattern with gold rims.

"Only she never uses them. She's afraid of chipping one."

"You sure don't take after her, do you? You're not afraid of anything. Broken plates, snow, sleet, cold, kids."

"Right," she said with maybe just a trace of irony in her voice. She wasn't afraid of having a plate broken. She was afraid of getting her heart broken. She'd said she was a big girl, that she could take his rejection, but she was not so sure anymore.

She looked at her watch. It was nearly time to meet the prince. Leaning against a kiosk, she pulled out her cell phone and called Meg to cancel their breakfast.

"You can't meet us because you're what?" Meg demanded.

"Having coffee with a prince," Sabrina repeated. "I'll explain later."

"This had better be good," Meg said. "For you to stiff us this way."

"I don't think we have a choice. It's like a command performance. You know how it is with royalty."

"I don't think I do," Meg said and hung up.

Back at the hotel, Sabrina and Zach decided to

change clothes for their meeting with Prince Frederic.

"What are we supposed to call him?" Zach asked, struggling with his tie in front of the full-length mirror in their room. "Your Highness?"

"In the movies, they say, 'Your Grace,' don't they?"

"Damned if I know. Wonder what we'll talk about."

"He'll probably say thanks for the room, and we'll say you're welcome. We'll drink a little more coffee, and that will be that."

"We're getting all dressed up for that?" he asked.

"Oh, yes. I forgot to tell you he thinks we're married. So unless you want to explain—you're Mr. White."

He shrugged as if he didn't care.

Sabrina shot him an appreciative glance. If he had no idea how divine he looked in his gray slacks and navy blazer, she was sure not going to tell him. Instead, she sat on the edge of the bed to slip into her burgundy three-inch round-toed shoes that matched her velvet suit.

"Hey," he said, his eyes gleaming. "You look good enough to eat…or to meet a prince." The look in his eyes made her flush.

They took the elevator to the penthouse. A tall, very slim man in a dark suit opened the door. The prince? No, too young, Sabrina decided.

"Ah, yes," he said with a brief glance at their attire, making Sabrina glad they'd taken pains to dress up. "Come in. His highness is expecting you."

Sabrina met Zach's gaze in a moment of acknowledgment. So the prince should be addressed as "Your Highness."

His Highness Prince Frederic rose from one of the straight-backed chairs to greet them. He wore a stiff white shirt, black vest and dark trousers. His face was lined and his thin gray hair was carefully combed over his scalp. He peered at them through wire-rimmed glasses.

"How good of you to come," he said in a frail voice. Frail or not, Sabrina definitely felt that she was in the presence of royalty. But he was not all stiff and formal. Over coffee and tiny, buttery pastries that he might have brought all the way from Romania, served at a small round table in the sitting area, he put them at ease by asking how they enjoyed the city and what they planned to do.

They mentioned the possibility of going to Alcatraz, climbing the Filbert Street Steps, visiting Coit Tower.

He gave them a few recommendations of places he remembered from half a century ago. It turned out the Palace of the Legion of Honor was his favorite art museum. In fact, he had donated several pieces to the Eastern European collection.

"But my most memorable moment in your fair city," he said, "was an afternoon spent in Golden Gate Park on Stow Lake. We rented a boat, my lady and I, and had a most delightful time. I remember it as if it were yesterday because it was there I proposed to her. These memories…" He shook his head. "Don't waste a moment of this precious time together," he said, fixing first Sabrina, then Zach with his watery blue gaze. "Make memories for the future when that's all you have left. Everything else turns to dust. My throne. My countrymen. My fortune. My wife and now my health. Everything but love. Love lasts beyond all else." The prince's eyes filled with tears, and the attendant who'd let them in signaled discreetly that it was time for them to leave.

Sabrina felt as if she should back out of the room with a deep curtsy, but she didn't. The attendant led them out, closed the door and followed them into the hall.

"You must forgive the prince," he said. "He lost his wife many years ago. But speaking of her today has brought back the memories."

"I'm so sorry," Sabrina said.

"Our apologies," Zach added.

The servant then pushed the button for the elevator, bowed and returned to the suite without another word.

"I feel so sorry for the prince," Sabrina said. "But, thanks to him, I know what I'd like to do this afternoon. I think Meg will understand we're busy."

After they'd changed clothes to jeans and sweaters, they picked up lunch from a deli on the street, then took a taxi to the park where they rented a rowboat at Stow Lake.

Along the shore were weekend artists with their paints and easels, as well as joggers circling the lake on the dirt path. They pushed off from the dock in their small boat, sitting side by side, each with an oar.

It was all Sabrina could do to keep from saying something like, "We make a good team." Or, "What kind of memories are we making?"

Instead, she admired the ducks waddling in the wake of their boat, waiting for them to throw crumbs. Zach pointed out the turtles who were sunbathing on the rocks and logs.

It was as if someone had declared a moratorium on sensitive subjects like love and marriage, sickness and health, and memories that would last forever.

As she plied her paddle in the water, she couldn't help but think of his brother's children. "The kids would love this, wouldn't they?"

"If they didn't fall into the lake," he said. "Brendan might be too scared."

"Lily wouldn't be. She'd have them all organized into paddleboats," Sabrina said with a fond smile.

They pulled up to Strawberry Hill at the center of the lake and beached their rowboat. On top of the hill, they ate their lunch while admiring the view of San Francisco with the sun shining on the silvery blue Bay.

It was all too perfect. Just as Prince Frederic said.

And all so transitory.

Chapter Twelve

Sabrina awoke Sunday morning, knowing their weekend was all but over.

They packed silently, then dressed, Zach in his slacks and blazer, she in her velvet suit, before taking a taxi to the Tenderloin district, the city's poorest area, to the Glide Memorial Church. In this multi-ethnic church, they sat in the pews with tourists, the homeless, the poor, as the choir belted out uplifting gospel songs. She and Zach shared a songbook and sang along with the other worshippers.

A sense of calm overcame Sabrina. She knew it was no good wishing for what she couldn't have. The best thing for her was to accept the good things that *had* happened to her. Zach being number one on her list.

It might have been the music, or the charismatic preacher, whose sermon was interrupted by applause and shouts of "Amen," or the other people in the church, but Sabrina felt totally connected to every one of them in a way she hadn't been to anyone for a long time.

"I don't know why I've never come here before," Sabrina said, feeling peaceful, as they filed out onto the sidewalk. "It's nothing like the suburban churches I've gone to."

Zach agreed. The music had stirred something inside him. The joy and the exhilaration of the people in the church was contagious. He took Sabrina's hand and they walked back to the hotel to check out. Just in time, too. Another few hours— another night with Sabrina—and he might have lost his determination to fade out of her life.

They drove in silence to her house, where he managed to say goodbye with only a brief kiss and no backward glance.

He didn't want to see the expression on her face. He hoped she'd gone inside to resume her life. A life without him.

In the car, he turned his cell phone on. There was a message from his brother.

"Sorry I missed your call, Al. I was in the city this weekend."

"What, you didn't have your phone with you?" his brother asked. "That must have been some weekend."

"It was." Zach didn't want to say any more. But he couldn't resist. "Sabrina and I had coffee with a prince."

"What? You and Sabrina and a prince? Wait till the kids hear about that."

Al was so excited he didn't ask any more about Sabrina. Thank God. If he had, it would have opened up a can of worms. Started Al thinking. Started Al talking.

"How are the kids?" Zach asked.

"Lily lost another tooth. Mary Ann drew a picture for you. Jenny wants to know when you're coming back."

"Tell them hello for me," Zach said, avoiding the question. He couldn't go back just yet. He had work to do. He had to get back into the groove. Back to being alone at night. Back to building up the wall around his heart.

"You have to come up for Michael's birthday."

"I'd like to, Al, but—"

"I won't take no for an answer. It's next month. Doreen sent you an invitation. Put it on your calendar."

"Okay. I'll try."

"Don't try. Come. The kids are counting on it. They talk about you all the time. You and Snow White. How is she, by the way?"

Al's casual tone didn't fool Zach. He was fishing. He wanted to hear that he and Sabrina were a couple. That they had plans for a future together.

"Fine. She's fine. I just dropped her off. But there's nothing between us, if that's what you're asking."

"Nothing but coffee with the prince," Al said.

Zach hung up, determined not to think about Sabrina. He tried not to remember how she'd looked first thing in the morning with two cups of coffee in her hands and a big smile on her face. He tried not to think about how she'd smelled like lavender, and how she'd looked with her skin glowing from a hot bath.

He forced himself to think about the guy she'd left at the altar. He knew how the poor guy must have felt. Dumped. Ditched. Deserted. That was what happened when you let yourself care about someone. Let yourself fall in love. You were vulnerable. There was no one in this world you could trust except yourself. There was no one who was obliged to be there for you when it counted. No matter what they told you. No matter what the songs said.

Zach, for one, would never be vulnerable again. He'd suffered enough. He learned his lesson early on and had never forgotten it.

In the weeks that followed, Zach did hear from Sabrina again, but only because Charlie's mom agreed to let Zach try to help her son.

Zach carefully avoided the school so he wouldn't have to run into Sabrina, and met Charlie at his house.

He refrained from giving the kid any advice. He just listened while Charlie talked. He was quite a talker. And he talked a lot about his teacher, Miss White.

He didn't know what the kid's problem was. After all, he still had two parents, despite their impending divorce, and a home. Twice as much as Zach had ever had. But sometimes it was eerie how much Charlie sounded like him at that age.

He'd also gone back to work with a vengeance. With some careful accounting, he found he was able to rehire the people he'd let go. Life was good.

Except there was a void. No use denying it to himself or anyone else. He missed Sabrina. He wanted her. He needed her.

It was a few days later when Zach pulled into the driveway of Al and Doreen's house, and noticed a strange car.

Before he'd even exited his car the kids came running out of the house and jumped all over him.

"Guess who's here?" Lily shouted, hopping up and down.

He didn't have to guess. He knew. *She* was there. And he knew what he had to do.

She came walking down the driveway wearing a fuzzy yellow sweater and dark stretch pants, and he felt a pressure around his heart.

"Hello, Zach. I guess they didn't tell you I was coming."

"I should have known."

Her mouth curved at one corner. Was that all the smile he was going to get?

"Can we talk?" he asked. He had so much to say. "I've been meeting with Charlie."

"I know. He told me."

"He thinks a lot of you," Zach said.

"You, too. You've done a lot for him."

"I haven't done anything. Not really. But seeing him, I saw myself. And I know that I'm not that kid anymore. I'm ready to move on. But I can't do it alone."

She nodded, but her attempt at a smile didn't really work. Her lips trembled. She said nothing he could take for encouragement. All she said was, "After the party."

Even as she spoke, cars pulled up in front of the house and children got out, presents in hand as they ran toward the front door.

The party was a blur of kids and noise. He didn't know why Al and Doreen had invited him. But he was glad they had. If they hadn't, he would have had to find some other way to talk to Sabrina.

He stood at the edge of the large backyard, watching Michael unwrap his presents, when Sabrina came outside with the cake. Michael made a wish, blew out the candles and Zach made his move. "I need to talk to you now," he said, after she'd cut the cake and Doreen dished out the ice cream.

She nodded and they left the party. He knew his

brother was watching him. He knew Al was probably poking Doreen in the ribs and that they were likely exchanging high fives. As if they'd arranged the whole thing. Which they had, hadn't they?

He and Sabrina found themselves walking toward the hill where they'd once played in the snow. It was now green and grassy under the springtime sunshine.

"I haven't called you," he began when they'd reached the top.

"I noticed." She sat down next to him and hugged her knees to her chest.

"You didn't call me, either," he said. "Well, not to talk about us."

"That was the plan, wasn't it?"

"Yeah, it was," he admitted. "I thought it would work." He glanced in her direction. Why didn't she smile? Why didn't she break down and tell him how much she was hurting, too? That she wanted him as much as he wanted her? He took a deep breath. It was now or never.

"But it hasn't. Not for me." He turned and looked at her. Looked deep into her eyes. She bit her lip. Her cheeks turned red. He took her hands in his. Her fingers were icy. He forced himself to go on. If he didn't tell her now, he never would. "The life I thought I wanted isn't good enough anymore. Not without you."

She put her hand on his arm. "Zach, don't say this unless you mean it. Unless you're willing to take a chance on me."

"On you? You're a sure thing. You're the best thing that ever happened to me. I love you."

"You love me?" Her eyes filled with tears. "You said—"

"I know what I said. I know what I thought. I was wrong. How do I know? Because if this isn't love, I've got a serious disease. I can't eat. I can't sleep. I can't work."

"That does sound serious," she said, her lips curving into a smile. "What can I do to make it better?" She leaned forward and kissed him, then pulled back to look at him.

"That helped," he admitted.

He put his arms around her. He kissed her the way he'd never kissed her before. Deeply, profoundly, forever. But, wait. There was something missing. He broke the kiss. Held her by the shoulders.

"When a man tells a woman he loves her, isn't she supposed to say something?" he asked. "Don't torture me, Sabrina. If you don't love me, say so. If you're still determined to retire as a shriveled-up spinster at sixty-five, tell me now so I can make other arrangements."

"What arrangements have you made?" she asked.

"None yet. But I was thinking of getting married at Al and Doreen's. In their backyard."

"With the kids all dressed up?" she asked, her eyes sparkling.

"I thought you'd like that," he said, pleased with himself. "But I can't marry someone who doesn't love me. Who doesn't want what I want."

"What's that?" she asked, wide-eyed. As if she didn't know.

"Kids, a house, a *home*."

"I love you, Zach. I fell in love with you the moment I fell through that front door. I tried to tell myself I wasn't ready for love. I have a terrible record. You know that. And you still want to marry me?"

"That's right, Snow White. I want to wake you up every morning with a kiss, like the prince in the fairy tale. I want to grow old with you and our kids. I want to be the father I never had. I didn't think I could do it, but—"

"I knew you could," she said, brushing a tear from her cheek. "I always knew."

"My all-knowing, all-wonderful Snow White." He kissed her again.

"Let's go tell the kids," she said. "Fairy tales do come true."

Epilogue

To Al and Doreen's delight and especially to the
delight of seven little kids dressed in their Sunday
best, the wedding did take place two months later
in the back meadow of the mountain house where
Sabrina and Zach had met.

It was summer in the mountains; wildflowers
covered the hills.

Sabrina's bouquet was composed of apple
blossoms, and before the ceremony she stuck a
flower in Zach's buttonhole. "For old time's sake,"
she whispered. "I still have the one you gave me

the night of the ball, pressed in the middle of my dictionary."

"Call me sentimental, but I kept the one you gave me, too," he confessed, and tucked a curl behind her ear.

"Hey, you two, time to take your places," Al said, beaming proudly at them. The musicians, friends of Al's and Doreen's, were tuning their guitars. "Everyone's in their seats," Al said, straightening Zach's tie, happily convinced that he'd finally repaid his brother for looking after him for so many years.

For only one brief moment did Sabrina think of that other wedding, so long ago. The one she'd walked out on. Thank God. This wedding was a complete contrast. She wore a simple white silk dress with a high neckline and long sleeves. There were only twenty-five guests. Her parents were there, looking pleased but slightly confused. Meg was there with Granger. This time, her attendants were the seven children. The girls looked adorable in pink flouncy dresses and miniature tiaras, their faces wreathed in smiles as they walked behind Sabrina, scattering wild rose petals on the grass. The boys wore crisp white shirts and dark pants, their expressions serious with the weight of the responsibility of walking the guests to their seats.

Sabrina had promised them they could be in her wedding, and today was the day she kept that promise. To them, to herself, but most of all to the man she loved.

When she vowed to love, honor and cherish Zach for as long as they both shall live, a sigh of collective happiness—and relief—filled the summer air.

Snow White had married her prince.

All was right with the world.

SILHOUETTE *Romance*®

To Protect and Cherish

by
KAREN ROSE SMITH

A gripping tale
of love and honor...

Anita Sutton needed a husband if she
wanted to keep custody of her children.
Her boss, Tate Pardell, felt honor bound
to protect her, so he proposed a
convenient solution. But as they were
pronounced man and wife, they entered
into an embrace neither could forget....

On sale April 2006

Available wherever
Silhouette books are sold.

SILHOUETTE *Romance*®

COMING NEXT MONTH

#1810 TO PROTECT AND CHERISH—Karen Rose Smith
A live-in housekeeper with three kids in tow! Sounds like a huge mess to jaded rancher Tate Pardell. Yet Anita Sutton and her kids bring luster to his days, and, soon, someone Tate never intended to hire takes his heart places he never thought it would go.

#1811 PRINCE INCOGNITO—Linda Goodnight
Tired of being the crown prince of Montavia, Luc Gardner only wants to remain out of the public eye. But one very determined and all-too-appealing private eye, Carly Carpenter, is on to him. Will her quest to crack a case lead to broken hearts—or help her find what's truly missing in her life?

#1812 DOCTOR'S ORDERS—Sharon De Vita
Thanks to a devastating romance with a rich, selfish man, Cassie Miller has sworn off love. That is, until she meets pediatrician Beau Bradford, who puts all her senses on high alert. Now does she dare listen to this doctor's orders and trust what her heart—and not her head—is telling her?

#1813 HIS QUEEN OF HEARTS—Roxann Delaney
Moments before taking her vows, bride Carly Albright walks out on her own wedding (who could blame her when she caught her future husband sleeping with her maid of honor?) only to discover that her rescuer, Devon Brannigan, might have ulterior motives. Now she must call his bluff to become his queen of hearts....

SRCNM0306